TWISTED MAGIC

KNIGHTS OF THE TWISTED TREE
BOOK ONE

BARBARA J. WEBB

TWISTED MAGIC

Book One of KNIGHTS OF THE TWISTED TREE

Copyright © 2024 by Barbara J. Webb

Book Cover Design by ebooklaunch.com

Cover art copyright © 2023

All rights reserved.

ISBN 978-0-9675066-4-7

To the survivors.

*K*ORIN STAGGERED OFF the boat with the rest of the passengers. The spring ocean had been rough, and he'd never managed to find his sea legs. Good to be on solid ground again, even if that ground was a city full of strangers in a foreign land where he was alone without a penny to his name.

Triome was said to be the greatest city in the world. It was certainly one of the oldest. Capital of Ritalle, the first kingdom, it was a center of trade, of knowledge, of culture, and also a sprawling, chaotic, mess. Most of all, it was a place to hide, where a person could disappear into the crowd. Even if that person was a wizard.

The docks already felt like an alien world, and Korin wasn't even in the city proper yet. His fellow travelers had been talkative, and Korin had listened, building a map in his head. He knew of the river markets where anything you could imagine could be bought or sold, the cliffside parks above where bright-plumed firstborn nobles crafted the futures of those who lived in the city far below. Of the great churches, large enough to house a village, with stained glass windows the size of houses and minarets covered in real gold. Opulent and vivid, crowded and alive, Triome was like nothing Korin had ever experienced. It would have been terrifying, if not for the greater horror he'd left behind.

The heat—Korin hadn't expected the heat. The spring air was muggy and thick. Locals rushed about in light, billowy clothes that would have been impractical—if not indecent—in southern lands. Half the men working the docks went shirtless, and the other half had collars dipping halfway down their chests. The women were in blousey, high-cut shirts that left their stomachs exposed, and slitted skirts that bared their thighs. Korin tried not to stare, but he'd never seen so much bare flesh.

Trying to escape it, his gaze travelled up. The docks sat at the mouth of the river that bisected the city. Across that river, atop sheer white cliffs, mansions like jewels glittered in the afternoon sun. Home to the firstborn nobility that ruled this city—this nation—these homes were nothing like the stark stone castles of the south. Even from here, Korin could see the gardens, the court-yards, the wide open windows and arching doorways. No frozen winters here. Or frozen falls and springs. Triome was beautiful and warm and alive, but Korin wasn't ready to call it paradise. Not yet.

The best thing Triome had going for it—it was as cosmopolitan as a city could be. No two faces here looked the same. Humans and firstborn alike ranged in color from pale and fair like Korin to skin so dark it was almost true black. Added into the mix were the coppery shades of the western deserts or the deep bronze of the northern coasts and all manner of in-betweens. No one stood out here. No one looked like they didn't belong.

The tiny mining town where Korin had spent his childhood had contained none of this variety, and the school at which he'd spent seven years hadn't been much better. The war had been—no, he didn't want to think about that.

Everything here was different, and if this was to be his home, Korin had a lot to learn. That would come later. First, he needed to get off the streets. The further he wandered out from the docks, the more his filthy, travel-worn clothes and half-starved appearance were starting to draw the wrong eyes. Which was any eyes.

He turned away from the cliffs and their shining palaces and aimed for the heart of the city. As the garish-colored buildings gave way to more sedate browns and grays, as he started to see more human faces than not, Korin knew he was where he should be. Now he just needed a place to stay for the night, and hopefully longer.

Korin ducked in and out of several different guesthouses, looking for a specific thing. Once he saw it, only then did he pull the necklace out from under his shirt and dare to draw attention to himself as he crossed the threshold and entered the busy tavern that took up most of this house's ground floor. He forced his shoulders back, making the most of his moderate height, and approached the woman behind the small bar who seemed to be in charge.

"Excuse me, ma'am?"

The woman he addressed was of that indeterminate age that could be anywhere between thirty-five and sixty, with reddish-brown skin and greying black hair pulled up in a messy bun. Her attention was on a thick ledger in front of her, although twice now she'd stopped what she was doing to pour drinks. She didn't seem to have heard Korin's soft words.

He tried again, louder. "Ma'am?"

"If you're needing a drink, talk to one of the girls."

"No, I don't—it's actually—a room. I need a place to stay. But I don't have any money."

That got her attention, and not in a good way. Her fists clenched as she stood full up. Taller than Korin. Her voice was loud, even over the din of the room. "Come in here wasting my time and interrupting—"

She stopped as her eyes locked onto the copper sigil at Korin's throat. "I see," she said, softer.

Korin kept talking. "I hope to stay in the city for a while. I can pay in trade. Can do any of the usual, plus I'm a healer. I can help any of your friends or family." He looked pointedly down at her hip, at the throbbing morass of pain he'd seen from the doorway. "I can help you."

She followed his gaze, and her mouth pulled tight as the words sank in. This was the critical moment, where she would either accept his offer or make some sign of prayer and scream for him to get out.

What she did was ask, "You drink?"

At Korin's nod, she turned back to the keg behind her and poured him a beer. "Wizard. And a healer, you say. Don't see many of your kind around this side of the city."

"Does this mean I can have a room?"

"Long as you keep quiet. I don't like noise and I don't like mess. You don't cause trouble, and you come through with the magic," her hand dipped down to touch her hip, then rose again. Korin didn't think she realized she'd made the gesture. "Guess if you do that you can stay."

"I promise." No noise and no trouble were at the top of Korin's current list of life goals.

"I'm Marta," the woman said.

"Korin." He took a drink of the beer. Watery, but not overly bitter. He'd tasted worse.

Marta looked him up and down, her hard eyes softening. "You hungry?"

"Starving," he admitted. It was no exaggeration. He'd barely kept any food down on the ship, and they'd been at sea for weeks.

Marta waved at one of the serving girls, who promptly disappeared into the kitchen. "How old are you, Korin?"

"Twenty-two." He knew he didn't look it. Not after the hard trip, with his shirt and trousers hanging looser than normal, making him come across like some kid trying to wear his grown-up brother's clothes.

Marta snorted. "I'd of guessed fifteen. Either way, you keep your hands to yourself while you're under my roof. The girls, they live here too, and all the work they do is with their clothes on, you hear me?"

Korin nodded quickly. "I wouldn't."

From under the bar, Marta pulled out a key. "Once Lily brings you back a plate, go on upstairs. Room number's on the key. I don't need you taking up a stool if you're not going to pay."

That was fair. And Korin was ready to be by himself in the quiet. "Thank you, Marta."

"There's a bath end of the hall. This early, you shouldn't have to fight anyone for it. And breakfast for boarders is served at sunup. Don't make me regret this."

"You won't." Korin could only hope to be able to keep that promise.

MUCH LATER, Korin lay in his new bed, the night's heat pressing down on him like a wool blanket, smothering. He'd stripped down to almost nothing and pushed back the sheets that had seemed so inadequate when he'd first collapsed under them. Exhausted from weeks of travel, of seasickness, of nightmares, sleep should have come easy. But this heat…this heat. Sticky and thick and wet, it was like nothing he'd ever experienced.

The sun had gone down hours ago, and Korin had thrown the shutters of his one, wide, window open, but even the soft breeze circulating through his room wasn't enough to alleviate the sense of being in an oven.

The heat wasn't the only thing keeping him awake. Now that he'd stopped moving, the memories—the guilt—that had stayed buried while he'd dealt with the more immediate questions of survival, those feelings were trying to smother him. Alone in the dark, listening to the strange night-noises of this new city, Korin could no longer keep them away.

Teriad. Lia. Jonathan. All dead, while Korin had managed to survive. Victims of a war they'd never wanted to fight.

Other faces. Strangers. Friends. People Teriad and Korin and Lia had tried to help. Other victims. The pain they'd suffered. Their cries as Korin had done what he could to save them. Their silences when he'd failed.

Teriad had believed in a better world. A place where, if you offered your hand to help it would be taken. A world where kindness won out over hatred. A world where one person's goodness could make a difference.

The war had taken that world from Teriad. From all of them.

The war was over now. The heroes had won the day. The villains were vanquished and buried with their blighted magics and conquerors' dreams. May they rot forever in their own cursed ground.

Teriad was gone, but Korin was alive. He'd escaped bloodied Ulek, made it to Triome, where the Wizard-Knight scourge had been driven out a hundred years ago. Korin could start his life fresh, return to the world Teriad had believed in. A world where he could help people like Marta. Trade healing for the modest lifestyle that was all he required. Offer his skills where they were needed, where they could do the most good.

Those thoughts should have been comforting. They should have been enough to relax Korin, to let him hope.

Except…

Teriad wouldn't have come to Triome. If Teriad had been here, he would have shaken his head, expressed his disappointment. No matter how many times Korin insisted Triome was the best place, the safest place. A big city where he could get lost in the crowd. A new start.

Teriad had been a good person, and had tried to teach Korin and Lia to be the same. "I can be that here," Korin whispered into the sweltering air. "I can be everything you wanted."

If there were other temptations here, sinister temptations,

Korin didn't have to give in. He was stronger than that. Better than that. He could be the wizard Teriad had taught him to be.

With that resolve firmly in mind, Korin was finally able to sleep.

LOUD KNOCKING at his door woke Korin in a breathless, sudden panic. Power sparked through his fingers until he remembered where he was. Remembered he was safe.

"Just a minute!" he called out, grabbing for clothes. The one outfit he owned was still damp from his attempt to scrub three weeks of travel out of it last night. It was clammy against his skin as he hastily dressed. Sadly once it dried, it would be too warm for this city and its omnipresent heat.

One of the girls from the tavern below was at his door with a tray of food, including a pitcher of orange juice that would have cost a month of his father's wages back in the south. The girl had the tray balanced on one shoulder, rather than held in front of her, which drew Korin's attention to the fact she was in one of those strange local dresses. Low cut at the neck, high cut at the ankles, and the soft brown skin of her stomach bared for all the world to see. After less than a day in this heat, Korin was no longer scandalized, and instead jealous at how comfortable that must be.

The girl smiled at Korin and gave a little wink. "Marta sent your breakfast up, since you didn't come down with the rest. She says once you've finished eating to come see her."

Korin nodded, understanding it was time to earn his keep. "Tell her I'll be right there."

He bolted the food, not wanting to keep Marta waiting. Plus he was still desperately hungry. The breakfast was strange—a bowl full of sweetened rice and vegetables—but delicious. And the juice: Korin savored that as much as he could. In his home town, they never had anything like this. In school, they'd had some slight better access to foods from warmer climates, but fresh fruit, or anything made from it, had still been a rare treat.

Korin took a minute at the small mirror on the wall behind his wash basin, frowning at his reflection. He wasn't used to looking so ragged. No wizard of the Staff should, but the time on the ship had been hard. He'd never found the trick of overcoming his seasickness. Hard to figure out new magic with his stomach roiling and his head dizzier than he'd ever felt in his life.

Because Korin was what he was, he knew the difference between exhaustion and real injury. A few days of good sleep and real food would repair the damage to his body. Once he'd physically recovered, he could worry about the rest.

He carried his dishes down with him and found Marta in a small office tucked behind the kitchen. He stood in the doorway, quiet, until she looked up and saw him. "There you are." She gave the same appraising look she had the night before. "Night's sleep did you good."

"Thank you." How bad had he looked before? "Is this a good time?"

"Good as any other."

Korin closed the door behind him. "Will we be interrupted?"

Marta shook her head, for the first time looking nervous in his presence. "You need anything? Any, I don't know, tools or supplies?"

Korin shook his head. "Just me. And I'll have to," this was the part that usually made people uncomfortable. "I'll have to touch you—where it hurts." Korin's hands were fisted behind his back. The wraps he usually wore had been so filthy and tattered, he'd had to throw them out. But he wasn't ready for the moment when Marta saw—when she would flinch away and no longer meet his eyes and then hurry him on his way like his hands were catching.

Marta stood up, turned so her bad hip was facing him. Completely at ease. She put her hand on the wall for balance, said,

"I tried to go to a wizard. After I fell. One of those black-robed fellows, with the animals."

"Order of the Wing," Korin answered automatically.

"Sure, right. Lots of their kind in the city. None a yours."

Korin listened to her talk with one part of his mind as another focused on his breathing, slow and relaxed, slipping into the right mental space for magic.

"He wanted money. More money than I ever had."

As Korin fell into a light trance, he once again saw the crackling red lines that ran over and through Marta's hip. The places it had gone wrong. This was what had drawn his attention last night. He'd seen the injury, known the pain it was causing her. She'd fallen, all right. She'd been lucky enough not to break it clear through, but Korin could see where it had fractured and regrown. Left like this, it was only a matter of time before the bones just snapped with age.

As Korin focused, the crimson lines grew clearer, run through with bright flashes of Marta's pain.

"Too much to ask those greedy bastards spare a little help for those of us who don't live posh."

If he stripped away the tendrils of pain, the lines of *wrong*, Korin could see the shape the bone had been. He could see how it was supposed to be. Clean and whole.

He lay a hand over the place that was broken. "This going to hurt?" Marta asked, her face turned away.

Korin couldn't pull himself out of the trance to answer. She'd know soon enough.

He'd found the truth of the bone, buried beneath the injury. The echo of what it had been for years, before that sharp, sudden change. A moment of sudden power, and the bone remembered.

Korin's mind grabbed at the memory, imposed it over the bad lines and snapped them together with a burst of will.

Marta gasped. Her hand locked over Korin's wrist; her nails dug into his skin. The pain of it was a distant awareness as Korin traced soothing energy through Marta's hip, fixing those little things that had gone astray. Torn capillaries, flesh, and tendons pulled and shifted. Another wave of power and he'd set everything to right.

He opened his eyes, looked up at Marta's tight face. "Better?"

She gave a cautious nod. "Yeah, I think. Hurt like the pit, but only for a minute." She bent her leg, flexed it, testing. "Feels fine now."

"Good." One night of sleep hadn't been enough to erase the exhaustion, or to dull the edges of grief and fear Korin had been holding back for days. This small act of aid, the thankful look on Marta's face, it was almost too much. He had to get away before he broke down. "I'll leave you to—"

Marta caught at Korin's hands. Turned them face-up, frowned. "What's this?"

Korin pulled free of her grip, gently, and closed his fists over the scars that rippled across his palms, made his skin into a patchy ragged mess. "An old injury. I'm sorry." The apology was automatic. So many people were horrified by the hands Korin used to heal them.

Marta shrugged, sat back at her desk. "You've got power, boy, no question of that. Don't matter to me what skin it comes through." She crossed her arms and the appraising business-woman from last night was back before him. "So, wizard of the Staff, new to Triome. Look like you're from the south, and you ain't got a bit of money on you. You running from something?"

Korin didn't try to lie. He was horrible at it, and Marta seemed like she'd be good at spotting them. All he could hope was that he'd earned himself enough good will for honesty. "Yes."

"Anyone chasing you?"

Again, he stuck to the truth. "I don't know."

She nodded with a satisfied look, like he'd answered more than she'd asked. "You got a plan?"

Korin shook his head.

Marta nodded again. "Figured as much. Well, I'm happy to make use of you, long as you want to stay here. I'd never turn away a wizard under my roof, even one of your kind. You've got lodging and all the food you can eat, long as you give help to any of mine that ask."

Korin wasn't sure what she meant by *one of your kind*, but, "That sounds fair."

Marta barked a laugh. "It isn't, not by a long shot. I'm taking horrible advantage. But there we are. Meanwhile," she unlocked a drawer with the key on her belt, rummaged around, and pulled out two silver coins. "Go get yourself some decent clothes. You'll melt in that wool shirt, especially once Spring really sets in."

Korin froze. The offered money was nothing Korin had asked for and completely unexpected. It was too much for his overtaxed mind to process. Marta rolled her eyes and grabbed his hand again, pressing the coins against his fingers until he took them.

Korin rubbed his thumb over the unfamiliar pattern on the coins' faces. "I don't know how much this is," he confessed.

"Light help you, boy. If you get through the day without getting robbed or swindled, I'll be amazed. That's two silver marks. If you stay this side of the river, that coin will buy you a couple secondhand sets of clothes with enough left over for a treat or two. Remember twelve pennies to a mark, as long as they've got the face of the dead King on 'em. Don't take any of your southern pennies as change. They go about half as far here."

"Thank you." Korin closed his fist tight around the money. His throat was thick with emotion. "I don't know—"

"None of that. Out you go. Some of us got work to do."

---

*K*ORIN SPENT THE rest of the morning shopping. On his way out, Korin had stopped to talk to Lily, the girl who'd brought him food last night. She'd been hard at work scrubbing the tavern floor, but she looked up at Korin and smiled, which gave him the courage to ask where was the best place was to spend Marta's money. Lily offered suggestions, then shyly asked, "You use your magic on Miss Marta?"

"I did." The way she continued to smile at him relaxed Korin. Some people freaked out about magic, even helpful magic. Nice to see Lily wasn't one of those. "Marta's going to be fine."

Lily nodded, like she expected as much. "There's some other wizards in the city who are healers, but they charge a lot. More money than we'll ever see."

Korin knew exactly what wizards she meant. "Wizards of the Wing. They're…" assholes, in Korin's experience. Arrogant, selfish, dangerous. "They're different than my order."

"The wizard who comes around here and does the lights and the sewers and stuff, he's nice. But he's got a different necklace than yours. It's purple, with a set of scales pictured on it."

"Order of the Balance."

"Right!" Lily answered brightly. "I remember that. And you're Staff. And now I know wizards of your order are much nicer than the Wing."

"I try." Uncomfortable with the attention, Korin excused himself from Lily and set out into the city to try to get through his first full day in his new home.

The wide square that Lily's directions led to was packed. To Korin's eye, it seemed like there were more people crowded in this space than the entire population of the town where Korin had been born. Which was both terrifying and reassuring. So many people Korin could drown in them, but also if Korin kept his head down, if he did nothing to draw attention to himself, there was a better than even chance he could live his life in peace here.

The storefronts around the square promised goods far nicer than Korin could afford, but the tables and stalls lined up outside were more reasonable. Everything was bright and colorful. Sparkling jewelry of cut glass, rainbows of dyed cloth, pillows and rugs, woven belts and painted sandals.

People all around him, just as bright. Just as colorful.

Some of them were wizards.

Korin froze at the sight of the Flame wizard, his heart pounding and mouth suddenly dry. The other wizard pushed his way through the crowd, unmistakable with his billowing sleeves of red and gold and the shining gold sigil around his neck. Even in this bright place, he stood out, but what Flame wizard didn't love drawing attention?

He was moving through the non-wizards, and no one seemed to mind. It was both terrifying and reassuring in a complicated mix.

There had been no wizards in the town where Korin had grown up. Then when he'd gone to school, it had been *all* wizards. When he'd traveled with Teriad, he'd been back to moving through a world where they were other, their welcome always in question. And then…the war.

This—this was exactly what Korin had hoped for. This was why he'd come to Triome. Wizards in the city, unremarkable among the masses. Two Star wizards negotiated with a glassware merchant—both dressed like Korin in dark, heavy clothes, but they were Star wizards so probably only passing through. Three tables down, a Crystal wizard argued with a metalsmith. No one so much as blinked. Just a part of daily life.

So why was Korin's pulse fluttering and his chest tight?

Needing something to distract him—to ground him—Korin turned to the closest stall. Fabrics in bright colors greeted him. He ran a hand along one, feeling its silky texture. They were well out of his price range, but the tactile sensation was soothing.

"Light," the woman behind the table muttered, the word a curse, and Korin jerked his hand back guiltily. Only after he looked up did he realize she wasn't looking at him.

Bright as a flock of peacocks, as subtle as a stampede of oxen, there was no mistaking a group of bored, young noblemen out slumming.

They were across the square, at a table covered with cut glass jewelry. Laughing, and not in a pleasant way. Korin couldn't hear what they were saying, but he recognized the contempt on the faces of the two men holding up various necklaces and sneering.

"What are they even doing this side of the river?" the fabric woman asked under her breath.

Korin's little mining village had been isolated and spent half its year buried in snow. They were probably under the claim of some noble family, but none of the nobles had ever visited. Likewise, at school, everyone had been like him—children of miners or fishers or tradesfolk. Once he'd graduated and apprenticed to Teriad, they'd kept to small towns and villages.

Only after he'd been drawn into the war had Korin met his first nobility and, on the whole, those meetings hadn't been pleasant. It was war. So little about it had been pleasant.

"Are they dangerous?" The question escaped before Korin could stop it.

The woman started, like she'd only just noticed him. "Not usually, but," she shook her head, still frowning. "It's been worse, with the prince away at the war. He took a lot of 'em with him. Ones left behind…" she shrugged. "Not the best of the bunch."

The young men were mostly firstborn. They were of mixed appearances: four men with hair and skin the soft brown and copper that seemed most common in the city. One dark brown, with hair to match. One particularly short firstborn, with bronze skin and sun-bleached hair. Two men as pale as Korin, one with blonde hair and the other with brown. And the last, tall and lean, with broad shoulders and sharp eyes and skin so dark he could have been first cousin to the royal family of Ulek. This last one hung away from the rest, a bored look on his magnetically handsome face.

Korin forced himself to look away, to turn his attention back to shopping. Staring drew attention, and the last thing Korin wanted was attention from that group. He touched the collar of his shirt, made sure his amulet was still hidden. Kept his head down.

After some amount of browsing, and more than a little haggling—Korin wasn't quite as helpless as Marta seemed to think —Korin had a couple pairs of light, drawstring pants, and three of the common open-collar shirts: one in bright blue, one in bright green, and one in bright yellow. Weird to think that in order to blend in, he had to dress like this. His only regret was he wouldn't be able to "accidentally" hide his sigil beneath his shirt.

Technically, it was illegal to hide the fact he was a wizard, to keep his sigil where no one could see it. Realistically, as long as he didn't do magic, he wasn't likely to get in trouble with it hidden. Here, where people seemed to welcome the wizards who walked among them, Korin's rational mind told him it was fine, it was safe, but it was impossible to pass that understanding on to the rest of him.

He also found a light pair of fingerless gloves that would keep most of the scars on his hands hidden. Just because he'd be wearing the sigil out in the open didn't mean Korin had to display everything to prying eyes.

The stall had a curtain he could change behind, and he took the opportunity—and the immediate relief—of the new clothes.

Korin spent the rest of his money on a delicious iced drink that was a mix of coffee and chocolate—two rare treats back home—and a guava pastry—a fruit he'd never before tasted. It was immediately added to his mental list of foods he needed to eat as often as possible. The last few pennies went to a little ceramic charm in the shape of a flower, to take back to Lily to thank her for her help.

The sounds of the market crowd had become a comfortable blur. But as the ceramic merchant handed Korin the little charm, carefully wrapped in paper, a sharp, shrill voice cut through the rumble. "What's wrong with his *face*?"

Korin's heartbeat sped and the taste of adrenaline flooded his mouth. Too on edge, too easily startled—Korin's knuckles went white against the bundle of clothes in his hand. Korin forced himself to breathe, reminded himself over and over—a mantra in his mind—that he was safe. That no one here was after him. That he didn't need to be ready to fight.

Risking a look back, Korin realized he'd let the group of noble troublemakers get too close. They were less than ten feet away, with only a scattering of people between Korin and them. Their attention wasn't on Korin, but that fact only provided him with a moment's relief until Korin saw who it was they'd surrounded.

An old man, begging. With gnarled hands and wrinkled skin and on his face—black lines. Black lines like rotting veins. Black lines spread like branches. Black lines Korin had hoped never to see again.

"Leave him alone," the dark, handsome one said. "Come on. I'm bored." But none of his friends were listening.

"Don't touch him," from the blonde, his voice laden with

disgust, as one of the others reached out to grab the terrified old man by the arm.

"What's wrong with him?" another of the group demanded.

Korin thought he knew. Korin had certainly seen this before. But the implications were terrifying if this poor old man was sick in the way Korin thought he was.

Either way, Korin didn't have it in him to just stand by and watch these highborn predators torture their victim. Keeping safe was one thing, but even Teriad would have stepped in to stop this. And Korin needed a closer look—needed to see if this old man was really carrying a disease straight out of Korin's worst nightmares.

Before Korin could act, the decision was taken from his hands. The firstborn who'd complained of boredom moved forward with the speed and grace of a striking cat, twisting his friend's arm so that his friend dropped the old man. The old man scrambled away with surprising speed, dodged between two of his tormenters, and ran off towards the edge of the square.

Korin didn't linger to watch any fallout between the firstborn. He needed to find the old man. He circled around the arguing group and dove through the crowd. Giving chase.

THE OLD MAN was shockingly spry. He led Korin away from the market, through streets of progressively-more-rundown houses, into a pocket of the city that seemed like another world.

This neighborhood had once been affluent. The boarded-over storefronts and crumbling houses were built with the same fine materials as the mansions up on the cliffs. They were twice the size of anything in Marta's neighborhood, and surrounded by little gardens and courtyards that were overgrown now, but had to have been beautiful once.

Every inch of it was abandoned. Like everyone had forgotten this part of the city even existed.

Understanding came into focus as Korin came around a corner

and saw the great marble archway at the end of the street. The grounds through the arch, left to grow wild. The remains of once-great buildings, now charred and broken rubble.

Before they'd retreated to their last castle stronghold in Ulek, before they'd started the war that had taken everything from Korin, the Wizard-Knights' seat of power had been here in Triome. Their academy had been one of the great jewels of the city, a place of knowledge and power from which they'd influenced the world, until they'd given in to corruption and greed. This was the first place people had risen against them, the first step of their long path down to destruction.

These ruins, wasn't this what Korin had come here to see? Wasn't this why he'd come to Triome rather than go anywhere else in the world? To spit on the graves of the dead who had brought so much harm to the world. It was a petty, petty urge and Teriad…

Teriad would have let it go. He would have turned his back on the war that was decidedly ended. Would have borne neither grudge nor regret.

Teriad had been a better man than Korin.

Korin had lost track of the old man, but now he was here, he couldn't look away. He needed to see more of the fallen academy, to touch the ruin, to reassure himself that the war and the horrors it had brought were over.

The Knights' Academy, alongside the school of the Balance and the royal palace, had been one of the three great landmarks of Triome. From here, the Knights' power had spread through the world. They had gathered here, built knowledge, counseled kings and queens. In its prime, the academy had been a center of learning, a voice of justice, a force for peace. Long ago, before the Knights had fallen.

Korin hadn't been alive to see the start of the conflict that had destroyed his family and broken his world. A hundred years ago, the war had begun when the King of Ritalle broke centuries of tradition to ally with the church and the wizard orders against the scourge the knights had become. The knights had been on the defensive ever since, their strongholds lost one by one, until all they had left was Ulek. Mighty Ulek, its royal castle high in the mountains. Ulek, one of the five great kingdoms. Ulek, where the King himself had been a Knight.

Ulek, where Teriad had died. Where Lia had died. Where Jonathan had died.

As Korin stepped through the arch, into the shadows of the great walled compound, the temperature dropped at least ten degrees. Korin tucked his shopping bundle into his shirt so his hands were free to pick up one of the crumbled bits of stone, and he threw it at the closest ruined building with all his might.

It felt good, that tiny jolt of violence. He'd fought so hard to stay calm the last few weeks. He hadn't dared draw attention to himself. He couldn't afford to let anything show. Not the anger, not the fear, not the deep, desperate loss.

Signs of the battles waged here still showed. Scorched remains of great stone buildings rose out of lawns thick with twisted weeds. Dead trees, warped and charred pointed up to the sky. It was nothing like the fields of Ulek, but Korin could feel the echoes of the same rotted magic, the same bloody fights.

The anger he'd been fighting, the pain, all bubbled up with a shocking suddenness.

"Your fault!" he called into the echoing emptiness. "All of it!" He marched forward, scooping up more rocks to throw as he went. More cracks in the stillness as his missiles struck the fractured marble and crumbling granite of the fallen buildings.

Bodies stretched out on the barren ground. Bleeding. Screaming. Wounds festering with oozing magic. Rotting skin. Soldiers catatonic after outsider spirits ripped away their souls.

It was the Knights' fault, and it had started here. At the center of the world.

Korin's arm ached from the unaccustomed exertion, but he

kept throwing. Rage like he'd never known. He wanted to hurt this place, to break it again. To destroy.

Angry boy. A whisper in the air around him. It was true.

Rage. Power. So pure. So perfect.

The voice swirled around him. Whispering. Caressing. Stoking the fire inside him.

Show them you will not be bound. Show them you will not be silenced.

How had he gotten this far in? And why was it so dark? The afternoon sun had been high in the sky. Korin's hand fell to his side and he took a step back. What was he doing? How did he—

A hand on his arm yanked him back against a broken column as the whispering voice dissolved into screeching, hideous laughter.

Another hand across Korin's mouth stopped his shout, and a new voice whispered in his ear, a voice backed by warm, living breath. "Hush."

Korin blinked as he took in his...attacker? Rescuer? What was happening? What had just happened?

He couldn't turn his head enough to get a good look, just an impression of dark clothes and dark skin, a tall man with high cheekbones and broad shoulders and...familiar, somehow.

"Come on," another soft breath. "With me."

The stranger kept a grip on Korin's arm as they crept back across the grounds. Unnatural darkness surrounded them, thickening to impenetrable blackness at the edge of Korin's vision. Like a viscous fog over everything, except that Korin could see just fine.

How had Korin walked into this?

They made it back to the arched entrance, passed beneath it, back into the heat and light of the afternoon. The stranger released Korin, turning to watch behind them. Korin looked too, but the grounds seemed the same as they had before Korin went in— shady, but sunlit, crumbling...*interesting*.

Korin fought the urge to return and deliberately turned himself away from the academy. Took his first good look at the man who'd dragged him out. Recognized him. One of the young noblemen from the marketplace—the one who'd stopped his friend from assaulting the old man.

"Some friendly advice," the firstborn stranger said with a strained smile, "if you're looking to commit vandalism, there are better—"

For the second time in ten minutes, the stranger grabbed Korin and shoved him back against a wall, but this time he pulled a knife and held it below Korin's chin as his other arm crossed Korin's chest. He leaned down—he was quite a bit taller than Korin—and the cold edge of the blade pressed just above the lump in Korin's throat.

The firstborn man's face was inches from Korin's, and despite the threat, Korin couldn't help but notice how attractive his attacker was. A sign of just how wrong everything was inside his head right now. The sharp edge of a knife poised to kill him, and all Korin could think about was the strong body pressed against his own and the sharp, handsome face glaring down at him.

"I'd better not see even a hint of magic in those eyes, Sunshine." The stranger's other hand gripped the sigil that had fallen free of Korin's shirt as they'd escaped. "What were you doing in there?"

Korin would have loved to have lived a life where this counted as the scariest moment he'd ever experienced. Sadly, it didn't even rank in the top three. "I don't know," he answered calmly, truthfully.

Dark brown eyes bored into Korin's. Searching. "You're a wizard of the Staff. You're trying to tell me you weren't in there riling those things up on purpose?"

"What things? What happened?"

"You really don't know, do you?" the stranger said in a low voice, like he was talking more to himself than to Korin.

Korin answered anyway. "I was curious. That's all. Next thing I know I was throwing things and yelling things and there were voices and it was way too dark."

"Place is haunted, Sunshine, and you woke it right the hell up." The man stepped back and slid his knife back into the sheath tied to his thigh. Korin spotted four more knives—three on the man's belt and one poking out of a tall leather boot—along with the slim sword hanging at the man's right hip.

He looked Korin up and down, his expression thoughtful. "New to the city?"

Korin nodded, daring to relax a little. "Just yesterday. I'm Korin, by the way."

"Ádan." He paused again, then seemed to come to a decision. "You drink, Korin? I can never remember which orders—"

"I do." Korin's mind had unfrozen enough to take account of his empty pockets and the fine clothes of the man before him. "But only if you're buying."

Ádan grinned, his face transforming into something beautiful. "Come on, then. I don't know about you, but I could use one."

As THEY WALKED, Korin took the chance to get a better look at Ádan now they had neither the crowded market nor unnatural darkness between them.

During the war, Korin had cared for enough firstborn to be intimately familiar with all the ways in which they were different from humans, and all the ways they were the same. On the outside, their bodies matched, in broad strokes. Two eyes, two ears, the same hands, arms, legs. Even if those eyes tended to be bigger, brighter, and those ears long and tapered. They could be beautiful in one blink, alien in the next. On the inside, it was different. Their structure was the same, but their bones, muscles, even their nervous systems were just different enough Korin had to learn different ways to heal them. Finally, magic worked through them differently.

Ádan was tall, like so many firstborn. He moved with an easy grace, and Korin couldn't quite take in all of him at once. He kept getting distracted by Ádan's muscular thighs, or his broad shoulders, or the way his thick hair shone in the sun, or…

Korin dragged his attention away from Ádan, focused on the street right in front of him. No good would come of these thoughts. Not now. Not ever.

Korin shook his head, trying to clear it.

"You okay?" Ádan asked.

"That place—the academy—it was unnerving."

Ádan's expression—not that Korin was watching—was at once exasperated and amused. "You didn't notice that *before* you went in?"

Korin chose to ignore that question. "How did you even know I was in there?"

Ádan glanced sideways at Korin, that same contemplative look as when he'd asked if Korin really hadn't known what was going on. "I noticed you in the market, saw you take off after the old man. I thought maybe he was a relative or something. I wanted to apologize. But then you went into the academy, and I thought you might need help. Had no idea you were a wizard."

"Are you saying you wouldn't have come in after me if you'd known?"

"Not without my sword out."

"When I was in there I—"

Ádan shook his head sharply. "Not talking about it without a drink in my hand."

Ádan led them to a bar with a bright sign above the door designating it The Sandy Fox. Despite the early hour, it was full of people talking and drinking and carrying on as though they had no idea their city was home to a haunted memorial to dead men. A number of the patrons called out to Ádan, who waved absently as he led Korin over to a small table towards the very back. The walls in this place were more window than not, and most were open to the breeze. It was certainly a different atmosphere than the dark, smoky taverns Korin was used to back home.

"So you're not from around here," Ádan drawled after giving a nod towards the man behind the bar. "You sound to me like a southern boy."

That Ádan had been listening close enough to Korin's words—that he'd noticed—it sent a little flutter through Korin. "All my life."

"Ulek? Aleton?"

"No. Nowhere you'd know. The little town where I was born, it was so far south I barely knew the color green, and I've never seen it on any map since I left. From there, I went to the school of the Crystal. After my father caught me playing with magic." Under the table, Korin's fists clenched. "Spent seven years at the school, earning my sigil."

Ádan gave a low whistle. "Seven years? Not bad. Most of the wizards I know were lucky to be through school in ten."

Korin felt a genuine smile spread across his lips. "What you have to understand, the tower of the Crystal is way up in the mountains, on the very southern edge of Torar. It's cold. All the time. The snow only melts for a couple months, maybe. During the winter, the sun all but disappears. Most of the school is underground, and that helps it stay warm, but that makes things even more claustrophobic."

Korin waved his hand around at the wide-open windows, the palm trees in the courtyard, the flowers growing along the window frames. "If I'd come to school in a place like this, I might have taken my time."

Ádan laughed. It was a warm, rich sound that washed over Korin and left his skin tingling. Which was no good at all, because developing an infatuation with local noblemen was *not* keeping his head down.

A petite blonde firstborn girl brought a bottle and two glasses to their table. She smiled at Ádan and he pulled out a gold coin, kissed it, then dropped it in her hand. She blushed and giggled. Korin felt an intense and unfair burst of jealousy.

Which was a clear sign he still wasn't okay. That a couple good meals and one night's sleep hadn't fixed him. That if, in the utterly unlikely event, Ádan might have brought him here for anything other than simple friendliness, Korin was in no place to even think about being anything other than friends.

Still, he wanted to understand what had happened back at the Academy. He waited until Ádan had filled their glasses with the honey-brown liquor, then said, "There was something in that place, talking to me."

"What did it say?" Ádan asked in a neutral tone.

The answer to that led in a direction that was way too personal. "Has it spoken to you? Do you know what's in there?"

Ádan sipped his drink, giving Korin another of those intense, considering looks. "You're the wizard. Why don't you tell me?"

This was far outside Korin's expertise. He had to reach back to half-remembered lessons from school. "You said it was haunted. But I don't think that's right. Whatever it was, it responded to me. Talked to me. Hauntings don't work like that. They're echoes, nothing more."

Ádan was watching Korin, one finger idly circling the rim of his glass. "So if it isn't haunted, what then?"

That was the question. More than just the voice Korin had heard, there was the old man and the sickness he seemed to have. "Could there be some lingering power of the knights? Some magic left over from the battles that happened there?"

Ádan drained his glass in one go, then poured himself another. "The knights were driven out a hundred years ago. That would be some incredibly powerful magic if it's hung around that long since."

"No worse than…" No, Korin didn't need to spoil this by talking about the war. "I wouldn't put it past them."

A strange little smile danced across Ádan's lips. "I'll defer to your superior education. All the same," he took another long drink, "I'd stay away from the place if I were you."

Korin wouldn't need to be told twice. "It's done." He lifted his glass and Ádan met it with his own. Korin took his first drink of the foreign substance.

Shepherd bless, it was strong. And sweet. Korin blinked against his eyes watering and sipped again.

Whatever his face looked like, it pulled another warm, buttery laugh out of Ádan. "Welcome to Triome, Korin of the Staff."

3

HE NEXT MORNING was devoted to chores around the guesthouse. Korin checked all the lights, re-enchanting any that were fading. Incinerated the sewage pit. Freshened the wards against insects. No serious magic, but all services Marta wouldn't have to pay for this month. It was nice to feel helpful, even if only in small ways. Or maybe best to feel helpful in small ways. It was the big ways that got you in trouble.

All the while, he tried not to think of Ádan.

They'd talked all through yesterday afternoon. Or rather, Ádan had talked and Korin had tried not to let show how much he loved listening. Ádan was funny, but more than that, he was smart and perceptive and the stories he told Korin about his adventures in Triome were so detailed and engaging Korin felt a little like he'd lived them.

When Ádan got excited about something, he started talking with his hands, those long, slender firstborn fingers dancing through the air like they were playing an instrument. Or when he was making a serious point, he'd lean forward, lowering his voice and looking Korin straight in the eyes. They'd killed two bottles of the rum, mostly Korin drinking, and that mostly to have something to do with his hands and his mouth so he wouldn't say or do anything embarrassing.

The first body any wizard of the Staff learned to diagnose and tend was their own, so getting drunk was never an issue for Korin. Although he had let the alcohol sink in enough to relax him and keep him a little tipsy. To keep him from thinking too much. After they'd parted—Ádan with a smile and a wave and, "I'll see you around, Sunshine,"—Korin had returned to Marta's feeling euphoric. Happier than he'd been in weeks. Months. Maybe ever.

His nice evening had continued after he'd come home. Marta had been at the bar, dealing with the early evening crowd when he'd come in. She hadn't smiled at him, but when she'd pointed him back towards the kitchen, he found a slice of honey-nut pastry set aside for him. And Lily had blushed and fluttered when Korin gave her the charm and thanked her for her help.

Last night, Korin had fallen asleep, not to memories of the cursed academy as he'd feared, but to the thought of Ádan's dancing sable eyes.

Korin recognized this all as the height of foolishness. Fantasies were fine as long as they remained fantasies. Ádan was nobility, and Korin was a wizard, and mere friendship between them was risky. To think about anything more—Korin should be smarter than that.

Except that Korin had never met anyone like Ádan. Not because Ádan was clever and charming and handsome and brilliant—although he had all those qualities and in greater quantities than Korin had ever encountered—but because he hadn't kept Korin at a distance. He knew what Korin was, and Ádan had liked him anyway.

This was another offense Korin could lay at the feet of the now-dead knights. As their seats of power had broken, as people had finally stood up to their evil, many of them had gone into hiding or simply gone rogue. They'd become criminals, thugs, bandits. People had become even more frightened, and that fear had blossomed into mistrust for anyone who might look anything like a knight.

Wizards, for example. Using magic or displaying your sigil had become a good way to get driven out of towns and villages. Korin couldn't count the number of times he, Teriad, and Lia had healed someone and then been sent on their way—sometimes apologetically, sometimes with threats of violence. Korin couldn't count the number of nights they'd been afraid to sleep without someone awake and on watch, always cognizant that offers of shelter could turn into a trap.

All because of the knights and their abuses of power.

Even Jonathan had taken a long while to get comfortable around Korin, and Jonathan's own sister had been a wizard.

At best, Korin met people like Marta, who was kind enough, but happy to let him go his own way. At worst…

No. Better to think about Ádan. About happier things. About the fact he might be able to make a home in this city. To have friends.

Lily and Verania were in the kitchen, cooking. The spice in the air was sharp enough to make Korin's eyes water, but it smelled delicious. The food in this city was amazing. Everything had so much flavor! It wasn't bland mutton or bland fish or bland reindeer. And if he never ate a blood porridge again, that would be more than fine.

It only took a little wheedling to get a waxed paper bowl of curried chicken and rice out of Verania. Korin left the guesthouse, eating as he walked, enjoying the afternoon breeze.

With his stomach full and no more chores to distract him, Korin's thoughts returned to the old man from yesterday. To those lines of decay threaded through the old man's skin.

If the old man had been the only strangeness from yesterday, that would have been enough for concern. Factor in what had happened at the Academy, and Korin had work to do. Even the smallest traces of the knights' magic lingering in the city could have deadly consequences, and no one else seemed to care.

His new clothes were much more comfortable in the sticky heat, although the open collar made Korin incredibly self-conscious. His burnished copper sigil with the raised staff hung right out there for people to see. He caught himself playing with it, covering it with his gloved hand.

But maybe because they were more used to seeing wizards here, when Korin could keep his hand down, he didn't draw near as many hostile stares as he feared. There were some frowns. A few folks very obviously changing their path to avoid him. Mostly, people seemed too busy with their own lives to bother with him.

The further he walked through the city with no one stopping to harass him, with no angry mobs, with no threats of violence, the more confident he felt. Enough so that before too long, his hands were comfortably at his sides and he was looking around, taking in the beautiful city, rather than staring at the street trying to avoid any eye contact.

Ádan had been a distraction, but now Korin had recovered his focus. If the old man's disease was what Korin thought it was—if that sickness was here in Triome—surely someone would have noticed it. Maybe even studied it. If that someone existed, Korin knew where he would find them.

Korin turned towards the tower at the heart of the city, a tower visible from the seaport, from the cliffs, from anyplace one cared to stand. Tall and graceful, reaching for the stars themselves, a tower of rose-colored stone with a dome of burnished gold at the top. The tower that was the center and focal point of the first and greatest of the wizards schools.

The Tower of the Balance. Korin was going to talk to his own kind.

. . .

ALL TOGETHER, there were nine orders of wizardry, with nine schools scattered throughout the five great kingdoms. Some were more prestigious than others, but each one offered essentially the same education—the foundations of magic that every wizard needed to know before choosing their specialty and joining an order. Most gifted children ended up at the school closest to home, but those who came from wealthy or otherwise privileged backgrounds could be sent halfway across the continent to go to what was considered a better school.

Korin's school had been small. The Crystal was remote and isolated, on the least populous edge of the least populated kingdom in all the world. The years Korin had been there, the most students they'd had at any given time was twenty, plus about half that many graduate wizards of the Crystal in residence to study their own arts.

The school of the Balance was nothing like that. The order of the Balance was one of the first orders created and carried all the status that history implied. It was a popular order, a wealthy order, and its Archwizard led the Council of Nine that governed all the wizards in the world.

Knowing and understanding were different things, though, and Korin hadn't been prepared for the sheer size of the place. He stood outside the gates, staring around at the campus, completely overwhelmed.

The tower alone was huge and could probably hold three schools of the Crystal just by itself. Surrounding it, across the sprawling grounds, were dormitories, classroom buildings, parks, and practice arenas. It was like its own little city in the middle of Triome.

And people. So many people. They couldn't all be studying magic. There weren't that many wizards in the world.

Korin's hopes and plans crumpled as he stared through the iron bars. Where would he even begin here? How many people would he have to talk to before he found out if they could help him?

It was too much. Korin couldn't do it. Not today. Not yet. In defeat, he turned away.

The streets around the Balance were full of storefronts, a number of them bearing wizard sigils. Not far from Korin's vantage point, there was a little shop with a sigil of the Crystal hanging over it. A flood of relief washed through Korin. The Crystal was home. After seven years around Crystal wizards, Korin knew how to talk to them, what to expect. And maybe the wizard in there would be able to help him navigate the school.

It was a strategic decision. He was choosing a different approach. Not hiding. Not at all.

He pushed through the door, into a well-lit, but cluttered shop. He could barely fit through the narrow aisles between shelves that reached up to the ceiling. The room was packed with utterly random assortments of knick-knacks. "Hello?" he called out.

"Hello!" a woman's voice answered from somewhere beyond the shelves. "Hello? Wait just a…hello!"

Korin homed in on the voice, made it through the maze to the back counter where a woman in a plain brown shirt and trousers with a white apron and a silver sigil around her neck leaned over a nest of copper wires she was working to detangle. She looked young, no more than thirty, but looks were deceiving with wizards. "Oh hello!" she looked up at Korin. "Have you been standing there long?"

"No, ma'am, I just got here." Korin couldn't help but smile. Her bright, curious eyes demanded it.

She sat up and pushed back the bits of long brown hair that had pulled free of her braid. "I'm Renée. Of the Crystal, obviously. And you must be new? I thought I knew all the wizard faces in Triome."

"Korin of the Staff, and yes, I just arrived."

"Pull up a stool, Korin." Renée looked around, frowned. "If you can find one." Korin didn't see anything that looked like it could be used for sitting, so he simply leaned against the counter. Renée nodded. "So what brings you to me?"

Korin didn't know what to do except be honest. "You looked friendly. And I'm feeling lost."

"Ha! Friendly, he says. That's one I don't hear often." She gave a cackling laugh. "So who or what wasn't friendly?"

"The Balance. The school, I mean. It's huge, and I have no idea where I'd go or who I'd talk to."

Renée's eyes were on Korin, but her hands were still buried in the wires, working strands free as she talked. "Just have to learn your way around, is all," Renée said. "Like anywhere. Where you from?"

That question had many fraught answers, so Korin picked the easiest one. "I graduated from the Crystal, actually."

"Ah, a boy with a real education. Good to know." Renée smiled, a smile with edges and teeth. "But it's different here. Bureaucracy. It's an ugly word. Everything's more complicated in a school this big, with more money than they know what to do with. You'll have to learn how to navigate it. Or…" she drew the word out, "you make friends with one of the faculty."

"Am I doing that right now?" Korin asked tentatively.

"We'll see." She winked. "First thing, tell me how old Perry's doing. Haven't seen him for years."

By which, Korrin assumed, she meant Archwizard Perrault, the head of her order and master of the school. Korin answered her the way he'd heard plenty of the Crystal wizards joke amongst themselves. "He's still got all his fingers and most of his toes."

"Ha! Well done. Now take some wire and make yourself useful while we chat."

KORIN SPENT a pleasant afternoon with Renée. She had known a number of his teachers, and was thrilled to hear any news or stories from the school. For most of the afternoon, they talked unin-terrupted.

It was strange, spending time with people like this. Yesterday, Ádan had done most of the talking, and that had been fine. Today, Korin was having to hold up his end. He'd almost forgotten how to do this when it wasn't about body counts and injury reports and what magic they needed to counter the day's newest horror.

In Triome, the war had ended a hundred years ago. People from this city might have gone to Ulek to fight, but it certainly hadn't affected the everyday business of people like Renée. For whatever value of business that seemed to be.

Korin observed that traffic seemed slow. Renée waved his comment away. "This is mostly just the place where I keep my stuff. My real work is special orders. Repairs. That sort of thing."

Korin finally took his leave as the evening light was turning sunset gold. Renée promised that if he came back in a couple days, she'd have a library pass for him and would be happy to show Korin around the school.

Triome was still surprisingly lively. Back in Torar, people would be rushing home, desperate to get inside before the sun set and the temperature plummeted. Instead, the streets seemed full of people meeting up, chatting, settling in at the benches and tables that were set up outside nearly every building.

"Look at you. Could almost pass for a local."

Korin jumped at the familiar voice. Ádan fell in step beside him. "That's a good shirt," Ádan continued. "The blue matches your eyes."

Korin had enough control over himself not to blush, despite the warmth that rushed through him that Ádan had noticed his eyes. "Where did you come from?"

Ádan shrugged. He had a half-dozen skewers of spiced chicken in one hand, nibbling at one as he walked. He offered one to Korin, which Korin accepted. "I saw you come out of Renée's. More shopping?"

The chicken was delicious, and reminded Korin how many hours it had been since lunch. "Just chatting. She's going to get me an introduction at the school."

"Oh, did you need one? That's easy enough to arrange."

Korin frowned, a reflex ingrained. The separation of magical authority and worldly politics was drilled into apprentices' heads for the entirety of their schooling. "How would you know anyone at the school?"

Ádan laughed, his deep, rich voice sending another ripple of heat through Korin. "This is Triome. The school doesn't only cater to wizards. The queen's own son learned his letters from the Archwizard."

A different world. Korin was going to have to remember that.

"What is it you need from the Balance?" Ádan asked.

"You remember that old man yesterday? The way he looked? I've seen that before. In the south. I need to find him. I need to know if other people are sick like that, and if any wizards in the city have tried to help."

Ádan passed Korin a second skewer, picking at his own chicken thoughtfully. "Those lines under his skin. You know what was wrong with him?"

"Maybe. I won't know for certain till I've gotten a better look."

"And you can help him?" Ádan's voice was softer now, sincerely curious.

"Maybe," Korin repeated.

They walked a full city block in silence before Ádan said, "Meet me back at the market tomorrow morning. I should be able to find him."

"You can?"

"Sure. I owe you that much to make up for my asshole friends yesterday." Ádan flashed Korin a wide, bright smile. "Besides, you're good company."

With that, Ádan split off, disappearing into the crowd. It took

Korin the entire walk back to Marta's to lose his silly grin at the compliment.

4

BREAKFAST WAS SWEET rice porridge and a whole orange all to himself. Korin was downstairs early enough to meet Marta's paying boarders, but after a few minutes of silence and nervous, suspicious looks, Korin took his food and fled back up to his room.

He'd talked Marta out of a double handful of candles and bag of salt with promises to look at her cousin's bad tooth. Other resources had been easily swiped from the kitchen. Lily had found him a small canvas shoulder-bag left by some previous boarder in which he could carry it all. Korin didn't know exactly what he was going to need, but these were basic tools, always useful.

For the last five years—ever since his graduation into the order of the Staff—Korin had travelled with Teriad, his teacher, and Lia, Teriad's other apprentice. Korin's time at the school of the Crystal had made him a wizard, but Teriad had taught him the deep secrets of their own order, had taught him how to be a healer like no other. Always on the move, through Torar and Aleton and finally Ulek. Korin and Lia had learned the hard way, with bloody hands and worn fingers and a growing knowledge of all the horrors that could be inflicted on the human or firstborn body.

Teriad had believed they had a duty to serve, to help anyone they could. As they travelled through lands growing increasingly violent in their fear and hatred of magic, nothing had tarnished his kindness or his faith. Even when he'd thrown Korin out, told him to leave and never come back, he'd done so in his soft, gentle voice and with tears in his eyes.

Korin closed his eyes, took a deep breath, and pushed those thoughts—those memories away. The same as he'd been doing for the last few weeks. He was getting better at it.

Ádan waited for Korin in the marketplace, a wide grin on his handsome face. "Morning, Sunshine," he said cheerfully.

What was it about this man that his smile drove deep into Korin to touch pieces of his soul he'd thought would be numb forever? What was wrong with Korin that he was so easily touched? Jonathan was dead. Teriad was dead. Had Korin forgotten them so quickly? What had he done to earn happiness?

With those sober thoughts in mind, he asked, "You found him?"

"I did. The old man's name is Dustin. He was a weaver—his family has a shop over closer to riverside. A few months ago, he showed up at the market, begging. Klie over there," Ádan nodded towards a table covered in fancy dyed cloth, "she gives him what food she can spare, got some of his story from him. Apparently, he ran off from his family when he started to get sick. Didn't want any of them to catch it. Now he spends his nights over towards the Academy ruins. Lot of empty buildings over there, but Klie pointed me towards a couple likely places."

As Ádan led, Korin considered the new information. That Dustin was just a man—no hint of magic in his background. That he'd started spending his time near the Academy *after* he'd gotten sick, not before.

"Penny for your thoughts," Ádan said once they'd left the crowded market behind and moved onto quieter streets.

What thoughts could Korin share? It seemed like so much of

his life had become wrapped in secrets. But they weren't secrets Korin wanted to keep. And Ádan was a friendly face—something Korin's life had lacked recently. There were some truths Korin could reveal without putting himself too much at risk. And it only seemed fair for Ádan to know what he was getting into.

"I came here from Ulek."

Ádan nodded. "I guessed as much."

Korin sighed. Ádan had guessed. Marta had guessed. He simply wasn't good at hiding things. "The old man, the way he looked—I saw that in Ulek. I saw..." His stomach clenched and his throat tightened. So hard to talk about this. But Ádan had to hear it. If he was going to help Korin, he needed to know.

So Korin came at it from a different angle. "They say Castle Ulek was one of the most beautiful places in the world, up there with Castle Darkivel and the Royal Palace here in Triome. Growing up, there was a woman in my village who'd been there once when she was a girl. She talked about it like it was made of magic. The gardens that covered the mountains. The fountains. The topiary dragons. Like magic," Korin repeated softly.

But he had to go on. "When we got there... My teacher, Teriad, he brought us there to help. When we got there, everything was already destroyed. Black and burnt and terrible. Nothing green left. The fountains and gardens had been torn up into battlefields. So much blood ground into the dirt that it had changed color. The smells—you can't imagine. The very air was greasy with smoke and grit and..."

This wasn't helping. As Korin paused to get control of his thoughts, Ádan said, "Prince Lysander's down there, along with a lot of my friends. I wasn't allowed to go."

"You're better off," Korin said. He'd been trying so hard not to think about this, to leave the war behind him. But Ádan was easy to talk to, and seemed genuinely interested in what Korin had to say. The words spilled out before Korin had a chance to second guess himself. "The knights turned to the worst sorts of evil magic you can imagine. There weren't many of them left—hundreds, versus the thousands that had them surrounded. But they held back armies of soldiers and wizards alike.

"They set loose demons. They raised the dead. All that was bad enough. Especially since the demons and undead didn't care who they killed once they were set loose. Ulek's own civilians were slaughtered along with their enemies. But that wasn't the worst."

Korin and Ádan had reached the decaying neighborhood that surrounded the Academy. It gave Korin a shiver to be talking about this so near the ruins of the Knights' seat of power. "I was never on the battlefield. We were there to be healers, nothing more. But I heard the soldiers talking about it. And from a distance, I saw them. The knights. How they'd corrupted themselves. Made themselves stronger, faster, tougher to kill. But the magic they used—it left its mark."

"The marks that were on the old man," Ádan said thoughtfully.

"Yes. Marks that shouldn't be there. Not in a city where the knights haven't been for a hundred years. Not this far from the war. Not on someone who isn't trained to magic."

Ádan had no response to that, and he and Korin walked the rest of the way in silence, each mired in their own thoughts.

They were in sight of the Academy walls when Ádan pointed Korin to an abandoned building that had once been some sort of shop with a tiny apartment above. The door was broken in half, the remaining part hanging tilted on its hinges, and Korin slipped through the gap. After the brightness of the morning sun outside, Korin was momentarily blind in the shadows, but as his eyes adjusted, he spotted the old man—Dustin—huddled in the far corner of the room.

"I don't have anything worth stealing," Dustin said in a small, resigned voice.

Korin approached him slowly, knelt down next to Dustin. "I'm a healer. I'm here to help."

"No help for me," Dustin whispered back.

Up close, Dustin looked even worse. The skin on his face was loose, patchy. The black lines that traced up from chin to forehead looked and smelled of rot. Korin had seen plenty of that on the battlefield. He knew blood poisoning, had seen diseased limbs rotting away. If this were a natural poison, with lines of decay spread this close to Dustin's heart, his brain, he'd be dead.

And as Korin sat studying it, the rotting lines rippled, and a new tiny branch reached out near Dustin's eye, spreading just fast enough Korin was certain it wasn't a trick of his eyes.

Korin took the old man's hand, sank his power into the old man's body. Brushed against one of those horrible tendrils and felt it pulse. It grew, sent out sticky feelers to wrap around Korin's energy, tried to suck him in.

Korin jerked back. No, this wasn't natural. Somehow the corruption the knights had invited into the world was living in this man.

"I need space to work," Korin said to Ádan. "A circle large enough Dustin can lie down in it. And there's a cup in my bag. I need it filled with drinkable water."

Ádan set to work. Korin stayed next to Dustin. "Does it hurt?" he asked.

"Like I'm being eaten alive."

"Do you remember anything that happened before you got sick? Were you near someone else who looked like this? Did you come to this part of town? Did you eat anything different, or hurt yourself somehow?"

Dustin shook his head to all Korin's questions. "Nothing different at all. Just woke up one day, and my hands were hurting and I saw the blight starting in my fingers."

Not much of a clue, but more than Korin had known before.

Ádan cleared the space Korin needed, then left to find water. Korin set to work preparing. He helped Dustin lie down where Korin wanted him, then pulled a piece of charcoal out of his bag. With it, he drew a circle around Dustin and himself, then a second circle, slightly larger. On the outside, he placed thirteen candles, equally spaced. In the ring between the two circles, he set out nine more. All the while he focused on his breathing, slowing it down, sliding into the relaxed, centered state he needed for serious magic.

When Ádan returned with the water, Korin directed him back to the supplies. "Take the salt—as much as you can mix into the water. It doesn't have to all dissolve. It just needs to still be fluid enough to drink."

Ádan made a face. "To drink? Really?"

Korin didn't answer. He didn't want to lose focus. He'd never done this on his own. For the first time, he wouldn't have Teriad watching over his shoulder, ready to save Korin if something went wrong.

Korin would simply have to do everything right.

Thirteen candles outside the circle. Nine within. "Pass me the cup." Ádan did so, silently. He watched Korin with studious curiosity, but Korin had no thoughts to spare for Ádan as he sank into his work.

Korin pointed at the first outer candle, lit it with a burst of power. One after the other, all around. Flames to keep the outside away. Then next, the inner candles, turning in the opposite direction. One for each order. The power of a wizard—his power—contained within the circle. If the magic went wrong, the circle would hold it in.

Dustin lay on the ground, his eyes wide, watching Korin. Korin dropped to his knees beside the old man. With one arm, he supported Dustin's shoulders to help him sit up. With the other, he held the cup to Dustin's lips. "Drink. It'll taste terrible, but the more you get in you, the easier this will be."

Dustin gulped, gagged, but got control of himself and managed to get through the full cup of gritty salt water. Korin lay him back down.

"Can I do anything?" Ádan asked softly.

"No." Korin stripped off his gloves. He wanted as few barriers between him and the disease as possible. He slid his hands beneath Dustin's shirt—one high on Dustin's chest and the other just below Dustin's sternum. He closed his eyes.

With his wizard sight fully awake, Korin could see the writhing wrongness that had invaded Dustin and spread through the old man like a tree setting its roots. The worst part was that the malignancy was moving with its own life, twisting and reaching and pulsing. The worst part was, it was as aware of Korin as Korin was of it.

The world fell away. All Korin knew was the body beneath his fingers. The evil within. Korin breathed in, breathed out, and with every exhale, sent magic into Dustin.

Not against the invading power. Not yet. First, he found the tiny grains of salt that were filtering out through Dustin's stomach and into Dustin's blood. A few pulses of Korin's power sped that process, hurrying it along.

Salt, pure salt, held magic like little else. As it moved through Dustin's blood, Korin pushed as much energy into the tiny grains as he could. To his open wizard-eye, a galaxy of glittering stars danced through Dustin, spreading and reaching until every limb and muscle and bone touched by the rot was also soaked in sparkling light.

The blight felt that power the same as it had Korin. Tendrils of decay reached for it, tried to draw it in. Except this time, it wasn't trying to pull Korin into itself, but Korin's weapon.

As it sucked in Korin's bait, Korin studied it. Watched it pulse and writhe. He'd seen disease that moved, that fought back, but never as active as this. Never so virulent.

Its eagerness was working against it. Hungry pseudopods surrounded the glowing grains of salt, consuming them. Pinpoints of light shone out through the darkness as it started to dissolve.

The blight pulled in on itself, trying to get away from the burning power. But Korin's magic had spread all through Dustin's body. There was nowhere for it to escape.

Thick lines of corruption, like grasping fingers, reached out of Dustin's chest and wrapped around Korin's hands and wrists, locking him in contact with the old man. Cold pain lanced through him where it touched, and it invaded Korin's skin, sinking into his own blood.

"Korin!" Ádan called out. Which meant he could see it. Like the lines on Dustin's face, this intrusion was visible to anyone.

Korin didn't have time to waste to wonder what that meant. Without understanding how it had happened, he was suddenly fighting for his life. He felt it, this pestilent, ravenous, decay as it moved through him like a poison in the blood. Invading and spreading with the speed of a wildfire. Oozing out his pores, trying to envelop him.

Another tentacle of rot reached out from Dustin, aiming for the circle. Trying to get out. And even worse, as it pounded against the inside circle, the candles on the outside guttered and dimmed. Something on the outside was trying to get in.

Korin, locked in his own battle, didn't have the energy or the focus to reinforce the boundaries. "Ádan! Get out! I can't—"

The thirteen candles flamed up with a sudden burst of power. Had Korin done that? He couldn't spare thought to worry about it. The outer circle was strong again and that was what mattered.

The corruption inside Korin threatened to consume him. But even as it surrounded and smothered him, Korin was studying it, learning the feel of it. How it felt moving through him. The taste of it.

He'd touched this magic before. Healed wounded soldiers with the dying remnants of this power still oozing through their blood. He'd never touched it while it was still alive and hungry, but those early encounters had taught him its shape.

He needed to focus. He knew how to fight back. Except it hurt so much. This blight spreading through him, scraping him away. His insides were rotting; Korin could feel it. Like his entire body was trying to dissolve.

Decay. Disease. Corruption. Yes, that was the key. Korin had faced all these things before. Never with such power behind them. Never so aware and malefic. Never so immediately threatening to his own life.

"Get out," Korin commanded the blight, hating how rough his voice sounded, how difficult it was to draw enough breath to speak. "You don't belong here."

Korin struggled against it, fighting to heal himself. Starting with his fingers, locking them in his mind. His hands as they were, without this violent invader. Inch by inch, piece by piece, Korin recreated himself as he had been before this disease invaded him.

Until the blighted power was a tight ball inside him, pulsing and squirming. Trying to regain its hold. Korin wrapped it in a globe of magic, fed it with a focused burst of healing energy, and smashed it into nothing.

Free, he could breathe again, move again. Healing Dustin was almost an afterthought. The blight had been in the old man longer, but it wasn't as virulent and aggressive as it had been once it had touched Korin. Whether it was Korin's young healthy body that had fanned its power, or his magic, Korin wasn't sure. But now he understood its nature, he was able to clear its weaker hold on Dustin.

Korin was free. Dustin was free. The blight was gone.

Korin collapsed.

---

5

*E*XHAUSTED, KORIN COULDN'T move. He was hunched over, eyes closed, knees aching from the stone floor. He couldn't even summon the energy to fall all the way forward.

Ádan helped Dustin out. Korin had no idea how long he was gone. All Korin could think about was breathing. But Ádan did come back. He crouched in front of Korin, their knees touching. "What was that?"

"Eaten alive." Those had been Dustin's words. They grated against Korin's throat. His whole body was in rough shape. But he was here, and the blight was gone, and the rest could be repaired.

He opened his eyes, saw Ádan's look of concern. "I'll be okay," Korin reassured. He risked a deeper breath. Rolled his shoulders to ease their stiffness. Opened and closed his hands.

Oh, but that was a mistake. Ádan was watching and his eyes went wide in an expression Korin had seen far too often. The same look Marta had given. Surprise. That would turn to revulsion. Or at best, distance.

Ádan caught Korin's left hand. Korin froze as Ádan gently pried open his fingers to look closer at the scarred flesh. Korin flushed, embarrassment and fear warring with something akin to desperation as Ádan's touched the shiny, rippled skin. Ádan traced his thumb over the rough lines, like a caress. "What happened?"

Korin was so mesmerized by Ádan's touch he answered the question rather than deflecting it. "My father."

Ádan's grip tightened; his finger stopped moving. Belatedly, Korin realized how that must have sounded. "No, not like that. He didn't…it wasn't his fault."

Ádan's movements resumed, a featherlight caress, tracing the scars, a contact that ran through Korin like an electric shock. "Tell me," Ádan said softly.

No one had ever touched Korin like this. Jonathan hadn't ever wanted to see the scars, and Korin had understood that. They were strange and ugly and Korin didn't want to make anyone uncomfortable. In the freezing south, Korin had gotten away with wearing gloves all the time. Even when he and Jon had…

Those thoughts hurt too much. Loss twisting around fear and betrayal and an anger Korin had no right to feel. So he refocused on Ádan, on the feel of Ádan's calloused thumb stroking Korin's palm, on the question Ádan had asked. "Our little mining town, we were isolated. Not big enough or comfortable enough for any wizard to want to live there full-time, and no reason for any of them to visit. When my gift started to show, no one was around to tell me what it was or what it meant."

Memories of that day were still bright and clear, even more than a decade later. "I was playing with the fire. Making shapes. It was—I don't know how much you know about magic, but the most dangerous time is always those early bursts of power. When you first realize the world around you is malleable. Or at least, parts of the world. Fire's an easy place to start."

"I've seen it happen, but up here it's different," Ádan said. "Not so many open flames around. Gifted kids play with wind and water. Rainstorms, if you can believe."

Korin could believe. In his time at the school, there had been horror stories of awakening wizards who had called down blizzards and worse. Yet another bad mark against wizards. "I was lucky I didn't hurt anybody. I was at the fireplace, making little animals out of the flames. A game. I thought they were pretty."

Korin reflexively clenched his fists at the memory, trapping Ádan's fingers in his own. Ádan didn't pull away.

"My father came in, saw...I don't even remember. A fox, or maybe a wolf. All made of fire. Next to me. He didn't know what it was, or that I was doing it.

"He grabbed the poker out of the fire. I'd left it there. He tried to...it was really very brave of him. He thought it was some sort of demon, trying to take me. He didn't understand it was just a game and I thought he was attacking my friend."

Korin closed his eyes. He could still remember the sudden sizzling pain. The strangely sweet smell of his own flesh burning. "I grabbed the poker, trying to stop him. It all happened so fast, neither of us were thinking."

Korin had immediately fainted. When the agony finally dragged him back awake, he'd been two days on the road, on his way to the school. "Father took me to the wizards to save my life. And they kept me there, knowing what I was. But there weren't any real healers at the school of the Crystal. They knew enough to keep me from losing my hands, but they couldn't fix me."

The worst part had been his father's guilt. How he'd barely been able to look at Korin after that. Korin had visited home a couple times during his school years, but he'd never felt comfortable, and his father had always seemed unhappier having Korin there in front of him, a physical reminder. In the end, it was easier not to go back.

"But you're a wizard now," Ádan said. "A healer. I don't...I'm sorry if this is insensitive; I don't mean to be but, why don't you fix them?"

Ádan wasn't the first person to ask that. Korin looked up, got caught in the liquid depths of Ádan's dark eyes. There was no judgement. Nothing but honest curiosity. And warmth. Like Ádan might honestly care. "The longer an injury's part of you, the harder it is to change. It's easy to set the body back the way it's supposed to be when the body remembers what that was. But I was a kid when I got hurt. Those hands don't belong to me anymore. These, now, these are mine."

Ádan's thumb pressed into Korin's palm as his eyes studied Korin's face. What he was looking for, Korin couldn't tell. After a long moment, he gave Korin's hand one last squeeze, then let go. "We should get you home, Sunshine. You look wrung out."

"I feel it. That was…I don't know. Blight—that's a good word for it. I thought it was some corruption the Knights were inviting into themselves, but it's not *just* that. This was malevolent and aware and…" Korin didn't know what else. It wasn't magic, not as he understood it. Or anything else he'd been taught about. "Hungry."

Ádan stood, offered a hand to Korin which he took, grateful. His legs were still shaky, but with Ádan's help, he found and kept his feet. "Did they create a weapon?" Korin asked, still mostly talking to himself. "Some power they summoned and lost control of?"

Ádan shook his head. "We should keep our minds open." A thrill ran through Korin at Ádan's use of *we*. "The dead are an easy scapegoat."

"They made it easy," Korin replied bitterly. "They went out of their way to soak up so much blame for everything, that blame started to rub off on the rest of us."

"Now that's hardly fair," Ádan said with a laugh.

Easy for him to laugh. He hadn't lived through it. By his own admission, Ádan had been here in Triome where the echoes and repercussions had long since faded away. "They're just a story to you. But I was there. I saw them. Ritalle kicked the knights out over a hundred years ago. For me, it's just been a matter of weeks."

"I know." Ádan was no longer laughing. Korin couldn't read the look on his face.

Not that Korin cared at the moment. "Don't tell me what's fair. Fair would have been if every single one of those murderers had been rounded up a hundred years ago, not just kicked out your door to be someone else's problem."

"I don't know if that's—"

"*It's their fault!*" Korin was yelling and he didn't care. "People are terrified of me because what I do looks too much like what the knights did. Master T-Teriad heals one broken farmer and suddenly we're all demon-worshipping boogeymen," that he stumbled over Teriad's name only made Korin more angry, "just like they were. It wasn't stories about the knights, it wasn't lies. And they're the reason..."

Korin was shaking. Still weak from the fight, far too on edge, he'd lost track of his better judgment. "You wouldn't understand," he finally finished.

"I guess not." Ádan sighed and his smile came back, although not as strong as it had been. "Come on. I'll walk you home."

THE NEXT MORNING, Marta's sharp voice caught Korin before he made it out the door. "Korin!"

He dropped his bag in the common room and went obediently to Marta's office. "You need something?"

"Sit down, boy."

Korin squeezed himself into the chair in the tiny space across the desk from where Marta sat, considering him. "So. You've been in and out and around the city. Verania says you fixed up her ankle. You stopped Lily's spring cough dead in its tracks. Holli's back doesn't ache anymore. Not to mention my hip and Eril's teeth. And that loudmouth delivery boy's blister. And all the magic in this house is running smoother than I've seen for years."

Korin couldn't figure out where she was going. "Yes, ma'am?"

"In all that, you seen any money past the marks I gave you your first day?"

Korin shrugged. "To be honest, I've never bothered much with money. When I was with Master Teriad, we simply traded for whatever we needed. There were always offers of food and clothes and a warm place to sleep."

Marta stabbed a finger at him. "You're in the city now. It's different here. You're going to need coin."

"I've been all right without."

"Hah! Not five days here and he's some expert." Once again, she unlocked the money drawer. Marta pulled out a small pouch and tossed it on the desk in front of him.

"What's this?" Korin asked.

"It's what I pay the wizards who come do those chores you took care of already." She paused, shrugged. "Well, half what I pay. You take it and do what you want with it." After another thought, she added, "Try not to get rolled soon as you step out the door."

"Thank you." Marta's gesture touched Korin. It was incredibly generous, even if she tried to pretend otherwise.

Marta waved him away. "Go on. I've got work to do."

Korin slipped the money into his pocket, retrieved his bag, and set out into the city.

It was a strange freedom to be able to wander where he liked, with no direction or obligation. His years with Teriad had been satisfying, but hard. And while Korin would give up this brilliant city in a heartbeat to have Teriad and Lia and Jonathan back alive, being here, on his own, was exhilarating in a way he never would have expected.

The idea of a bed that was his, night after night. That he could walk out the door without worrying about whether he'd be able to find the next village or the next shelter before sunset brought killing cold. Teriad had pushed them hard, but with good reason. They had to survive.

Now Korin had food and shelter. Even if Marta unexpectedly

evicted him, the weather here was so comfortable, a night on the street wouldn't be the worst night he'd ever spent. The city might be huge, but it wasn't the vast wilds of the south and Korin couldn't wander far enough that he couldn't make it back home. For the first time in years, Korin was able to look past the questions of survival and think about what he *wanted* to do.

Then of course there was Ádan.

He'd brought Korin home yesterday, made sure Korin got safe to his room. Korin had simply fallen into bed and gone right to sleep, his body desperate for a chance to recover from the blight that had tried to invade it. When Korin had awoken, refreshed, in the early afternoon, he'd found a note on top of the tiny dresser by the door.

Feel better, Sunshine.

That was all. But it had sent a flutter through Korin, a complicated wave of hope and fear and longing.

Korin knew it was foolish, this crush on Ádan. Maybe even dangerous. But like everything else about his life here, Ádan was so unexpected and so bright, almost magical.

It was all so impossibly complicated. Just thinking about Ádan made Korin smile, but that happiness brought its own upset. What had Korin done to deserve to be happy? Didn't he owe Teriad and Jon and Lia more of his heart, his devotion? They were gone and Korin was already trying to forget them. What was wrong with him?

He should walk away from Ádan. He should focus on magic, on helping people. On atonement.

He absolutely shouldn't be heading towards the Sandy Fox, the bar Ádan had taken him to that first day. That place where they had so clearly known Ádan that he must be a regular.

When had Korin gotten so bad at doing what he should?

Barely to lunchtime, and the Sandy Fox was full of patrons.

This city was nothing but crowds. He stepped in a little ways—not enough to get a waitress's attention, but enough he could scan the tables for Ádan.

No. Not here. But as Korin turned to go, a hand fell on his arm. He tensed, turned to see a well-dressed man with red hair and freckles and eyes the color of the ocean. Pearl buttons down his shirt and a gold-inlaid scabbard at his side and Korin was pretty sure this was another noble. Possibly a friend of Ádan's.

A possibility confirmed when the man said, "You're Ádan's new wizard friend, right? Korin?"

Korin nodded, relaxed a little, although the man's grip on his arm didn't loosen, and a part of Korin's mind couldn't help but feel that hold was a threat.

Even more intrusive, the man reached up with his other hand to touch the medallion at Korin's neck. "You're easy to spot."

Warring desires surged through Korin. On one hand, the fact Ádan had been talking about him made a melting pool of warmth in Korin's stomach. On the other hand, he wanted *away* from this stranger who was too close, who was touching him uninvited. But if this was one of Ádan's friends, he didn't want to be rude.

Korin took a deep breath, trying to sound natural as he asked, "Have you seen him?"

"Oh, I'm sure he'll be around." The man flashed a conspiratorial smile. "Pretty thing like you, how could he resist? Now I see you, I get it. Truth be told, I was pretty surprised. To hear Ádan say he was slumming around with a wizard."

Korin's entire body short-circuited. "Slumming? What?"

"It's not like him, you know?" The man was still grinning, like they were sharing a joke. "Usually he knows better. Believe me—I can't tell you how often I've heard him and the prince go on and on about wizards and their magic. Filthy stuff. Can't trust it. But I have to say, you seem to be something special."

"I...what?" Korin could barely form a coherent thought.

"You have to understand. With the prince gone, everyone's a

little bored. Who can blame Ádan for looking for some extra-curricular entertainment? Some new way to kill time?"

This—this right here was the treatment Korin was used to. This was the prejudice he'd been expecting all along. But Ádan had tricked him. Lured Korin in. Got him to lower his guard. And now...

Now it hurt far more than it would have if Ádan had said these things to him at the start. "I have to go," Korin said, his voice surprisingly calm to his ears. Like it was coming out of someone else. Someone who wasn't betrayed and angry and suddenly sorry he'd ever come here. He jerked back, and this man—this *friend*—let go just as Korin pulled, so Korin stumbled back through the door.

And of course, because the universe hated Korin, Ádan was here, standing in the doorway, blocking Korin's retreat. "Korin!" Ádan greeted him brightly.

Korin wanted none of it. He pushed past Ádan, or tried to. Ádan was tall and solid and didn't give way. To Korin's horror, he reacted with anger-driven reflex and a burst of magic to give extra strength to his shove. Ádan stumbled back, and Korin fled.

Hating Ádan.

Hating himself.

6

TIK. TIK. TIK.

Korin opened his eyes, held his breath. The sound came again.

Tik. Tik.

Something against the shutter.

Korin crept out of bed and over to the outside wall. Pressed flat, so he wouldn't be visible from the outside.

Tik. Tik. Tik.

Tiny stones against the wood. Korin leaned over, cracked the shutter open, looked out.

Ádan was in the alley with a handful of gravel. He stopped mid throw as he saw Korin's face. He smiled.

Korin slammed the shutter closed.

This wasn't happening. Except that it was. Why was this happening? What had Korin done to deserve it?

Korin slipped downstairs, out the door, around back to the alley. Where Ádan was still standing, waiting. Still smiling.

Korin wanted to hit him. Instead he asked, calm as he could manage, "What are you doing here?"

"You seemed upset earlier. I thought we could—"

"No." Korin cut him off, as pissed at Ádan's chatty tone—like they were friends who'd just run into each other on the street—as he was at everything else that had happened that day. "*What* are you *doing* here? Are you bored? Slumming with me and my *filthy* magic?"

Ádan flinched and the smile vanished from his face. He stepped forward, raised his hand like he was reaching out for Korin, then pulled it sharply back. "Oh no. No, Korin. Where did you get that idea?"

Korin crossed his arms, glared. "Your friend at the bar told me exactly what you've been saying behind my back."

"What? No!" This time, Ádan came all the way to Korin and put his hands on Korin's shoulders, holding him there as Ádan talked. "I would never say anything like that. What makes you think I would?"

Woken out of deep sleep, in the middle of the night, Korin's mind wasn't turning at full speed. And Ádan's touch wasn't helping. The warmth of his skin that had so quickly transmitted through the thin fabric of Korin's shirt. Korin pulled himself free before Ádan's closeness distracted him too much. "He doesn't even know me. Why would he lie?"

Ádan's answer was slow and careful. "Nikki has never…he doesn't like that I'm friends with you. He doesn't like people like you."

Korin's confusion was clearing into anger. "People like me?"

"Wizards."

Exactly what Korin expected. "And what about you, Ádan? How do you feel about *people like me*?"

Ádan's eyes swept down and back up Korin's body, and his wide smile just about short-circuited Korin's brain. "Sunshine, if all people like you were people like you, I'd drag them home and never let them out of my sight."

Ádan couldn't possibly be saying what it sounded like he was saying. It didn't matter how much Korin wanted to hear it. Just because Korin had a lonely, desperate emptiness inside him didn't mean it was a good idea—a safe idea—to pretend Ádan wanted anything but friendship.

Even friendship was dangerous. Could Korin trust Ádan? Which was more likely—that Ádan was telling the truth? That Korin had randomly stumbled onto one of the few people in the world who didn't harbor any sort of fear or distrust of magic? Or that Ádan's friend—who, yes, was probably acting on his own agenda—had *also* been telling the truth about things Ádan had said?

Was Korin ready to take that risk? After everything he'd been through, was it worth inviting so much more pain on the tenuous hope that Ádan truly was everything he claimed to be?

Ádan gave him a quizzical look, studying his face. "Korin, what's wrong?"

Which was too much. "Oh my good god!" Korin yelled, "Did you honestly just ask me that?"

"Shhh." Ádan held up a hand, looked up at the other windows that opened onto the alley. "You'll wake people." He stepped in close again and Korin had to brace against softening his posture one little bit. He would not, did not welcome Ádan's proximity.

"We should go somewhere," Ádan said. "I can apologize some more."

"You haven't apologized yet."

"Well then, we should go somewhere and I can apologize. And we can talk. But we can't keep out in the street all night."

Korin had already been out longer than he wanted to be. "I can't. I have to sleep. I have to sleep, in my room, like a normal person who has a room and needs to sleep."

"Another time, then." Ádan flashed Korin another smile that, despite all Korin's best efforts, made Korin's whole body tingle. "Good night, Korin." He gave Korin's shoulder a friendly squeeze, then slipped off down the alley, disappearing into shadow.

Korin trudged back up to his room and returned to bed, hoping that the light of dawn would bring sense to everything.

It didn't.

Sunlight through the open shutter roused Korin from his fitful sleep. From dreams of himself and Ádan in the alley, in the darkness. Dreams where Ádan's smile had twisted into something cruel and mocking, where Nikki's words had come out of Ádan's mouth. Dreams where Ádan hadn't been alone, where Teriad and Jonathan had stood behind him. The names they'd called Korin had been even worse.

It had been so easy to be angry at Ádan because that kept Korin from having to be angry with himself. Yesterday, in the doorway. Just because it had been a harmless shove didn't make things any better. Korin had acted without thinking, used angry magic against someone. He wasn't safe to be around. Not safe for Ádan and not safe for himself.

What Korin needed was to stop thinking about Ádan, and to that end, he had a plan for the day. Korin hadn't forgotten Dustin. The man was healed, but he'd picked up the blight somehow, from somewhere. If that magic, that infection was in Triome, Korin needed to find it.

Even this early, Triome was awake and bustling. Korin fell in with the moving crowd, kept his head down, tried to avoid attention.

Until a familiar voice said, "I'm sorry."

"What?" Korin looked up, surprised, almost tripped.

Ádan caught his elbow, steadied him. "That's what I should have started with last night. I'm sorry."

Had Ádan held on to Korin longer than was necessary, or was

Korin so focused on every casual touch that they seemed to go on forever?

Oh, Light, he was in trouble. "You're not forgiven." But the words didn't have the energy to be convincing.

"What Nikki said was terrible, and I know you have no reason in the world to trust me. I don't know how to prove to you that I'm not like that. But..." Ádan's voice lowered, his tone now utterly serious. "There's something bad happening in this city. We both saw it. And no one else seems to care."

Even harder to believe than the idea that Korin had found the one non-wizard who was completely comfortable with magic was the idea that he'd randomly stumbled across a nobleman concerned for the health of people in his city. "You're telling me you want to help track down the blight."

"Was that in question?" The familiar cheer had returned to Ádan's voice. "So where are we going?"

"I suppose it does me no good to say you aren't invited."

Korin expected a quick retort, but there was only silence from Ádan. When he looked over, Korin had to stop walking, his entire attention drawn to the serious depths of Ádan's dark eyes. "Do you truly want me to leave you alone?" Ádan asked softly.

The rational answer was *yes*. The answer that belonged to this new life, a life of keeping his head down, of staying safe. But the word caught in Korin's throat. He couldn't say it, not caught in the trap of those beautiful eyes. "I'm going to talk to Renée. She's been in the city longer than me. I'm hoping she might have some idea of how to start looking."

Ádan broke the eye contact. A good thing, or Korin would have stood like that all day. Ádan waved his hand forward, gesturing for Korin to precede him. After only another moment's hesitation, Korin started walking again and allowed Ádan to follow.

7

*R*ENÉE WAS AT her workbench, slotting tiny gears into an unidentifiable device like she was building a puzzle. She looked up, her eyes huge behind the goggles she wore. "Welcome back Korin. And…" She squinted. "I know you. At the school, about ten years ago. One of those hellions that ran around with the prince. Family…family…zhi Dhari, right?"

Ádan nodded. "But please, ma'am, just Ádan."

"Yes." Renée drew out the syllable thoughtfully. "You and Prince Lysander. Troublemakers, the lot of you. Although as I recall, when those other lackwits weren't looking, you were a sharper student than you wanted to let on. Could have made a wizard out of you, if you'd had the gift."

"No thank you." Ádan smiled and winked at Korin. "I'm happy to leave wizarding to others."

Renée rolled her eyes, a gesture made comic by magnification. "And what brings the two of you in here?"

"Library pass?" Korin reminded. "You said—"

"Oh! Yes. I have it. Somewhere." Renée pulled off her goggles and started rummaging through drawers and cabinets full of clutter.

Ádan pulled up a stool and settled in next to the workbench. He looked perfectly relaxed, comfortable in the presence of two wizards. But then, Korin had yet to see Ádan ill-at-ease anywhere. "I thought any wizard had free access to the library," he said, watching Renée dig around.

"Of course they do," Renée answered without looking up. "But the school still likes to know who's coming and going. The Archwizard pays attention to who's making use of the resources."

That thought spurred a flutter of an idea. "So they would know if there are any other wizards of the Staff in Triome?"

Renée sat up, gave Korin a sympathetic look. "Sorry, kiddo, but I can't tell you the answer to that one."

So much for that brief flash of hope. Another Staff wizard would be able to help Korin figure out the blight. Would be able to help Korin figure out a lot of things. "The city's huge. Are you sure?"

"I'm sure. Believe me. The Archwizard keeps a close eye on the city. No offense, Korin. You seem like a good kid. But your order's got a poor reputation."

"Why? What could anyone have against us? We're healers."

Renée raised an eyebrow.

Ádan said, "It has to be an utterly unreasonable prejudice. Just look at Korin."

"Thank you." The words were inadequate to communicate the heated gratitude Korin felt at Ádan's defense, but they would have to do.

Ádan continued after flashing a grin that sent warm shivers all through Korin, "The point still stands: no other Staff wizards in the city means no help with the blight. Unless you think one of the Wing wizards might be able to come up with something."

Korin and Renée snorted in unified derision. "Wing wizards, useless lot. All of them," Renée said. "But what blight are you talking about?"

Korin explained about Dustin, from his first glance of the man in the market square to his struggle to heal the aggressive, invasive, blackness. Ádan added in details. Renée listened, nodding along. When Korin was done, she asked, "So you think this has to do with the dead knights?"

"Yes," Korin said.

At the same time as Ádan answered, "It's too soon to tell."

They looked at each other and Ádan shrugged. "Korin's the expert," he amended.

"I don't know," Renée said. "This is way outside my expertise. I can see why you'd want to consult with someone in your own order."

Korin hadn't really expected Renée to know what to do. But it was disappointing to hear anyway. "What about other wizards who were in Ulek? There were plenty of us around. Surely some of them were from Triome."

"Well sure," Ádan answered quickly. Earning him a wry look from Renée. "Of course Wizard Renée would know better than I," he continued, managing to almost sound contrite.

"Most that went fighting are still down there. The few who've come back—couple Flame wizards, couple Sword wizards. Even if they noticed this sickness of yours, they're not going to have figured out anything to do with it. Except kill the poor bastards who have it."

Which meant Korin was truly on his own.

"Aha!" Triumphant, Renée pulled a folded piece of heavy paper from a mixed stack of envelopes, wires, and other scraps. "Here it is. One library pass."

"Thank you." Korin tucked the paper inside his shirt.

"And I'll be happy to give you a tour myself, but not today. I promised Lord zhi Elias I'd have this music box ready for his wife's birthday, and I'm horribly behind."

"I know my way around the school," Ádan offered. "If you need a guide."

And that settled that. Renée waved them away, her attention

already back on her own project and Korin followed Ádan out of the shop.

PASSING through the gates of the school of the Balance with Ádan, Korin couldn't remember why he'd been afraid to come on his own. It was big and crowded, sure, but friendly enough. And Korin was a wizard. He belonged here.

"I think I'm getting used to the city," he said, which drew a quick smile out of Ádan. It still amazed Korin how easy Ádan smiled.

"I love it here. I wouldn't want to live anywhere else." Ádan nudged Korin with his elbow. "I'm glad you're settling in."

In the end, the school of the Balance was no different than the Crystal. It had classrooms, just more of them. It had students— many, many more of them. The wizard faculty were more of a mix than Korin had seen in the south. The Crystal school had employed mostly Crystal wizards. Here, while there were plenty of wizards wearing the deep purple sigil of the balance, the halls and grounds had just as many Book, Flame, and Star wizards, with a scattering of Sword and Eye. No other Staff, as Renée had said, and if there were any Crystal wizards here other than Renée, Korin didn't see them. No Wing either, which was interesting.

Korin wasn't surprised to find the Balance had a far better library than the Crystal, which was exciting. Teriad had never been much of a scholar, preferring hands-on experience to magic theory. Now that Teriad was gone, Korin was going to have to be in charge of his own continuing education.

Ádan proved a tireless research assistant. Once Korin explained the sort of texts he was looking for—books and pamphlets on disease and anatomy, particularly anything that had been written here in Triome in the last hundred years—Ádan turned out to be better at navigating the stacks than Korin.

In all, they spent hours combing the library. First focused and productive. Later laughing together as they stumbled across obscure tomes with strange titles like *Varied Philosophies of Caterpillar Organization* and *Lumber in all its Uses: an Autobiography*.

Ádan walked Korin home, each of them carrying an armload of books. Ádan dropped his stack in Korin's room, then lingered in the doorway. "That should keep you out of trouble for a while."

A certain spark in Ádan's eyes that was dangerously familiar. Or maybe it was the way he leaned in when he spoke, like Korin was exerting some sort of gravity. "You think I need keeping out of trouble?" Korin tried to match Ádan's teasing tone.

"No question of it." Ádan took a half step forward. Towards Korin. Not quite crossing the distance between them.

The signal seemed unmistakable. Except that this was Ádan— handsome, charming, kind Ádan who was too perfect for words and how could he possibly want Korin? It was too much Korin's fantasy, impossible to believe. And if he was misreading, if he drove Ádan away…

But Ádan was so close. All it would take would be for Korin to reach his hand up, to lean forward, to finish closing the gap. Korin had wanted this since he'd first looked into Ádan's eyes.

Except that even if Ádan really was indicating interest, even if the impossible was true and Ádan wanted Korin, did Korin even deserve that? What did it say that he was so eager to make time with Ádan when Jonathan was less than a month buried? How shallow was Korin? How selfish and callow?

Ádan deserved better.

After an endless minute of Korin standing frozen, Ádan quirked a little smile. "Don't stay up too late reading, Sunshine." He turned on his heel, graceful enough to make it look like that was what he'd intended all along. Left Korin standing there, confused and alone and hating himself.

Whatever else might be true, there was one thing Korin knew for certain.

He was a coward.

8

*I*T ALL CAME back to the Knights.

The blight was tied to them. There was no other answer.

He shut the book he'd been studying—what was essentially the diary of a Wing wizard who'd lived in Triome a couple hundred years ago. The wizard had kept exceptional notes on his magical studies, as well as on various diseases that had moved through the city and a couple cases of victims of magical attack.

This was the final book in the stack he and Ádan had brought back from the library. Korin hadn't found any mention of disease, poison, or affliction of any sort that was anything like the blight. That, along with the undeniable evidence that he had *seen* the knights in Ulek with similar-looking symptoms, made the conclusion inescapable.

But how? The affliction of the Knights had been tied to their magic. It hadn't been a disease in the usual sense. Korin had seen no signs that it could spread. On the warfront, in direct proximity to the blighted knights, there had been no one like Dustin.

But here in a city thousands of miles away, a city where the

Knights hadn't set foot for a hundred years, the exact same affliction had struck an old man with no ties to magic, the Knights, or anything that should have made him sick in that way.

It was late. Korin had been reading for hours. But his mind was too spun up to consider sleep. Frustration with this mystery made him restless. He couldn't bear to sit in his room any longer.

His last visit to the abandoned academy hadn't gone well, but Korin had walked in without expecting trouble. If he went back now, he'd be better prepared. And the very fact that the place was still so energized suggested there were secrets to be found.

Some lingering pocket of corrupted power—even that didn't sound right, but it was the best idea Korin had so far. It was a tempting narrative, and certainly a thing that happened in stories, but Korin was a trained and educated wizard. He knew—*knew*—magic didn't work like that.

Magic was complex and challenging. There was a reason that, even after ten years of school and several more years of apprenticeship, most wizards spent their lives engaging in nothing more challenging than the sort of small-scale, domestic magics that kept the world running. Keeping lights on and trash burned and pipes clear and houses safe. Important, but relatively simple tasks. Bigger magic was complicated and hard. To reach beyond that, to start picking apart the workings beneath all the rote tricks and familiar processes...

The first lessons a wizard learned used familiar things as analogies. Think of magic as water, of its flow. Think of magic as fire, the way it spreads. Think of magic as lightning, that strike of power. But none of that was true.

Magic didn't spread like fire. Magic did nothing of its own. If magic changed something, it was because some intent behind the magic wanted that thing to change. If magic corrupted something, it was because some intent behind that magic wanted a thing corrupted.

So what was the intent behind the blight? What was the intent lingering in the knight's academy? And the most important question of all—who was driving it?

Triome at night was quieter than Triome during the day, but there were still a surprising number of people in the streets. Korin kept alert, but no one approached him. This was one situation where his wizard sigil kept him safe. Only the most desperate of criminals would risk accosting a wizard.

By the time Korin reached the academy, the moon had sunk behind the walls, and the grounds were buried in shadow. Korin fed a trickle of energy to his sigil, made it glow. Enough light he shouldn't trip over anything, but not so bright as to call attention —he hoped.

Korin took several slow, deep breaths. Settling into a not-quite trance. His wizard sight was wide open. Thus prepared, he stepped through the open gateway and into the academy.

As before, he felt prickles of anger rise inside him, but this time he recognized the impulse as not his own. Alert and aware, Korin could feel the tingling pressure moving through him, like poisoned air. Dry, dead grass crunched under his feet and the desiccated branches of dead weeds and shrubs seemed to claw at his legs as he pushed through them.

Teriad had talked to Korin and Lia about hauntings and curses and other magics that could make a place go bad, but he'd never offered more than broad theory. Teriad had believed their time better spent healing people, not places. There'd always been an unspoken implication that too much time spent on cursed ground could corrupt even the best wizard.

Spirits, or fragments of spirits, could get trapped in the world. Or could be bound, intentionally. Those hauntings couldn't really talk to you. They were echoes of a person that used to be, not the person themself. Once disentangled, they were quick to dissipate. Spirits didn't belong in this world and never wanted to stay.

Curses were stories told by people who didn't understand magic. Like the fields around Castle Ulek, that would be known as cursed ground—probably for centuries—but what it was, was magic used to torture—the land, the air, the people—that had left behind its own pollution. It would be toxic, but not alive. Not aware.

Not talking to him.

Korin had heard a voice—an actual voice. One that had seemed to know him. Dustin's affliction had been too complicated —too dynamic, too alert—to be nothing but the result of contact with poisoned magic. Even the worst sort of poisoned magic.

Something was going on here. But what?

About a hundred feet in, Korin stopped. He was in the center of what once had been a wide-open lawn. Parade grounds or practice fields, flat and empty, now overgrown with twisting, choking weeds, as many dead as alive. Korin closed his physical eyes, reached out his arms, stood still, and waited.

With his eyes closed, Korin's other senses woke up. The rotting smell of death. The unnatural silence. And to his wizard senses, the presence of a heavy, creeping power.

Korin focused on the power, but didn't move. He felt it reaching for him, surrounding him. A tingling presence, tiny tendrils of it poking at his flesh, up his legs, around his chest. Pressing against him, trying to get in. Like the power was trying to take root.

Power like he'd felt inside Dustin. Power unlike what he'd felt inside Dustin. The same and not the same. As Korin stood here, it presented no immediate danger. Maybe if he stood here a week, a month, or maybe if he—

A sudden blow to the small of his back sent Korin sprawling. He landed hard in the weeds, felt them cut against his face and his arms. The force of his landing made him bite his tongue and he tasted blood. He scrambled up to his knees, looked for his attacker.

Nikki stood a few feet away, cloaked and hooded in dark grey and nearly invisible in the dim light. He had a sword in one hand and another rock in the other. "Hello, Korin," Nikki said, and threw.

9

THE ROCK WHISTLED by Korin's ear, missing him by inches. Korin flinched away, watched it strike the ground, which was all the distraction Nikki needed to close the distance between them. A rough grab at his shoulders and a push and Korin fell backwards again to the hard ground. Then Nikki was on top of him, a knee pressed against Korin's chest and Nikki's sword across his throat.

Korin's calm focus had shattered and the strange power around him responded. The whispering voice from before had returned. *Fight back. Danger. Kill him. So easy.*

Korin dug his fingers into the cold, brittle ground and tried not to listen. "Get off me."

The sword pressed closer, its sharp edge denting Korin's skin. "Make me," Nikki answered.

Yes. Make him. Kill him. Strike out.

Like the ground here knew him. Knew what Korin could do— what Korin had *done.*

All the nightmares, the fears, the anger, flooded through Korin like a burst of adrenaline. His hands twitched, power at the ready. He *could* strike. Nikki was right there. Korin wouldn't have to move. He could tear Nikki apart, inside to out, before Nikki knew what was happening.

He will bind you. He will hurt you. Fight back.

Another voice. Teriad's voice. The memory as clear as if Teriad were here beside Korin. "I'm sorry, but I can't forgive this. I can't forgive you. Go away. Now. I can't teach you anymore."

"No," Korin said. To Nikki. To the whispers. To Teriad. "No, I won't."

"What are you doing here?" Nikki leaned down so his face was inches from Korin's. His sword kept an even pressure against Korin's neck, just shy of what would break the skin. "You don't belong in this city. You're not wanted here. We don't need you."

He'll kill you, the voice whispered. *Fight back. Fight back.*

"You may have Ádan fooled, but I know what you are."

It was too much. "Get *off* me!" Korin backed the words with power, shoved Nikki away and scrambled to his feet.

Nikki rolled like a cat and was instantly up, triumph in his eyes. "That's it. There you go. Show me what you're really made of."

Now he was standing, without a sword pressed to this throat, Korin's mind started churning again. Coming up with questions. "What are you doing here? Are you following me?"

"What are *you* doing? What do you want with Ádan?"

Was Nikki jealous? Was this something else? "I don't see how my…" Korin stumbled for the right word, "how Ádan and I are any of your business."

"Ádan's my friend, which makes him my business. And I won't stand by and watch him be used and betrayed by someone like you."

Strike now, while he doesn't expect it. Korin shook his head against the voice. "What are you even talking about?"

Nikki pointed his sword at Korin. "You're lurking around a graveyard in the middle of the night. No, not just lurking. You were doing something, *wizard*. Were you listening? Did you hear something?"

"I'm here for a reason." Nikki's accusations cut too close to the bone. "A good reason. I'm trying to help people."

"Of course you are."

Frustration, anger, and—yes—fear pushed Korin's voice louder. "I *am* trying to help. And not by ambushing people in the middle of the night in a place...You call this a graveyard, but it isn't. A graveyard is something you build to honor the dead. The dead here, they don't deserve honor. They don't deserve respect. This place is *wrong*, and somehow, despite the fact the knights have been gone from here for a hundred years, they're still creating victims."

"Victims." Nikki took a step forward. The tip of his sword was shaking. He wasn't in any better control than Korin, which made him dangerous. "You want to talk victims? You're so happy the knights are gone, but you think your kind aren't just as bad?

"Let's talk about a town that doesn't exist anymore because, after they threw out one of your kind, every single man, woman, and child fell to the plague. Let's talk about the man who begged me to kill him because he'd pissed off a wizard and couldn't sleep for the nightmares that came every time he closed his eyes."

Korin had heard stories of bad acts. There were always a few stories. Which made the horrific rumors and people's fears even harder to fight. "Those were abuses. They shouldn't have happened. I'm not like that. My order, I'm a healer—"

Nikki laughed. A dark, bitter sound that echoed against the Academy's crumbling stone walls. "Healer? Really?" He took another step forward so the point of his sword rested against Korin's breastbone. Korin braced himself, but didn't move.

"Do you even know your own order, Korin of the Staff? Do you know why there's not a single one of you in Triome? Do you know the body count you *healers* have racked up? Do you know why people are terrified of that sigil you wear?"

"Stories," Korin said with more confidence than he felt. "Exaggerations. It's because of the knights. People see magic and they think… I'm not…" *like that*, he meant to say, but he couldn't get the words out. Not with Teriad's voice still echoing in his head. *I can't forgive you.*

Nikki's smile was bitter. "You're not what? Go on. Tell me what you're not like. Tell me if I dug deep enough, that I wouldn't find *stories* about you. Tell me you're innocent. Stand there in the darkness that reaches for you like a brother and tell me another lie about how you're not the monster the world thinks you are."

It was too much. Nikki's words, Korin's guilt, and the maddening whispers rising up from the blighted ground. Korin took a step back.

And ran.

It was the middle of the night, so of course Renée's shop was closed, but Korin pounded on the door until a light came on in the little second-floor apartment. A moment later, Renée leaned out the window. "Light bless, Korin. Do you know what time it is?"

"Please, I need to talk to you."

"Of all the…" she pulled her head back inside, still muttering, but the locked door clicked open beneath Korin's hand.

Renée's apartment was every bit as cluttered as the shop below, full of books and loose sketches and half-finished clockworks and stranger machinery. Renée was in her tiny kitchen, grumbling as she set a pot of water on the stove. "No talking till I've had some caffeine."

Korin paced while Renée saw to her drink. She watched him, her face gradually softening. Finally, with the scent of fresh coffee hanging in the air, Renée settled in the one available chair and said, "All right. You want to talk, so let's hear it."

"I need to know about my order."

Renée sipped her coffee, her eyes on Korin, studying him. "So you just woke up in the middle of the night and decided you needed a history lesson?"

"I'm not joking."

"Neither am I. As the aggrieved party here, I think I deserve a little more of an explanation."

Korin had to remind himself that Renée hadn't caused any of the frustrations or fears that had wound him into this state. That yes, she absolutely deserved some consideration for taking him in at this hour and agreeing to talk. "Earlier today, when I was in here, I said Wizards of the Staff were all healers, and you gave me this look, like you didn't agree. And then just now…"

It took very little time to give Renée the details of his night, his encounter with Nikki. He told her everything. Nearly everything. When he talked about the cursed academy, he left out the voice that twice now had spoken to him. Korin finished with, "Is what he said true? About my order?"

Renée sighed, leaning her head back against the chair. "Your Teriad, I can't decide if he was a saint or an idiot."

"Renée—"

"Hush, Korin. You came here to ask me questions, now let me talk."

Except she didn't. Renée sat in silence, staring at the wall above Korin's head, lost in her own thoughts. Korin had stopped pacing, but as the silence stretched on, his nervous energy grew until standing still was almost unbearable.

When she spoke, it wasn't anything Korin expected. "Why did you join the Staff?"

The answer was easy. "Because of Teriad."

"But why? Are you telling me that if a Star or Flame wizard of sufficient charisma had been around you would have joined them?"

"No. No, I never…" It was hard to think about. All his memories of Teriad now had jagged edges, ready to cut. "Teriad visited the school a few times while I was a student. There was one particularly bad winter where he got snowed in for about a month. I was still learning fundamentals at that point, but he'd sometimes hang out in the commons in the evenings and talk to the more advanced students about magic. Staff magic. And he talked about helping people.

"I liked listening to him, because it seemed to matter to him, what magic could be used for. He wanted to use it to help people. He talked about responsibility and care and it all made sense to me. It was exciting and interesting, and when I asked Teriad if I could apprentice with him once I graduated, he said yes."

Renée nodded. "So you didn't actually know anything about the Staff before you committed yourself."

"Archwizard Perrault—well, you know how he is. He didn't believe in 'gossip.' We learned about the nine orders, of course, but mostly we focused on the sort of magic they did."

"Not what they chose to do with it," Renée finished. She set her cup down, then steepled her fingers, resting her chin on them. "Korin, you have to understand, there are bad eggs in every order. The Council of Nine is supposed to police that sort of thing, but...but we live in the real world. The Archwizards have their own agendas. Most of the rest of us, we're just trying to get through the day.

"Look, a lot of orders have their reputations. People get nervous when Flame wizards are around. No one trusts wizards of the Eye. But, yes, there are reasons for that. And reasons why your order makes people uncomfortable."

"We're healers," Korin insisted.

"*You're* a healer. And it sounds like Teriad was too. But you tell me—is that all your magic can do?"

The room was suddenly too hot and Korin couldn't look Renée in the eyes.

She didn't wait for his response. "You're a smart kid, Korin. I knew that the first day you came in here. And it sounds like you're good at what you do. Doesn't take much thinking to figure out that what you do to heal people can be flipped around to hurt them. And that's the easy—the obvious. Really dig into the magic and there's some seriously creepy shit your order can pull off that none of the rest of us can even start to figure how it's done."

"Stop," Korin said weakly.

"You asked. And now I'm telling you. Like I said, people get nervous around Flame wizards because sometimes when you piss them off, things blow up. But that's nothing but a fire hazard. Staff wizards, your magic digs into the places where nightmares come from. And yeah, there are plenty in your order—too many—who are eager to find that place."

I can't forgive this. I can't teach you anymore.

"I'm sorry," Renée said in a kinder tone. "I can tell this isn't what you wanted to hear. But truth is all you get in the middle of the night."

"No, thank you. And I'm sorry."

"Go home, Korin. Get some sleep. If you want to talk more tomorrow...today...I'll be here."

KORIN LET her shoo him out, but as he emerged from the shop, Korin stopped. And stared. Because Ádan couldn't possibly be there, leaned against the wall, waiting for him. Could he?

At the sight of Korin, Ádan pushed off the wall. "Nikki told me you two had a fight."

"Is that what he said?"

"Yeah. I was a little suspicious, given the hour and the fact I haven't seen you running around randomly picking fights with people." In the pre-dawn darkness, Ádan was mostly shadow, but Korin could tell that, for once, Ádan wasn't smiling. "Are you alright?"

"No," Korin answered honestly.

Ádan nodded, like he'd expected the answer. "Come on,

Sunshine. There's a place I want to show you. Best view in the city."

Korin let himself be led. They moved south through the sleeping city. To the river and across, then up a series of steep paths that led to the bluffs. This was the wealthy part of Triome, where the houses were more like palaces, and the streets were lined with parks and courtyards. Ádan seemed completely at ease, guiding Korin with purpose. He knew exactly where they were going.

Down a couple side streets, still climbing. Until Ádan took Korin's arm to pull him into a little park, the entrance of which was nearly overgrown with flowering bushes and that Korin never would have seen on his own.

The bushes opened to lush grass and a marble fountain and a view of the entire city and the ocean beyond. They stood at the top of the bluffs. With Triome so far below and the thick vegetation behind, he and Ádan could have been the only people in the world.

Ádan sat down cross-legged in the grass and leaned back against the fountain. "This park belongs to the crown. It's one of Prince Lysander's favorite places."

"Should we be here?"

"It's fine. With Lysander down south, no one's going to bother us."

What must it be like to be able to walk into a place like this, confident you belonged? But that was Ádan. Everywhere he went, he seemed at home. Korin had yet to see him uncomfortable or ill at ease. It was more than just confidence. Korin had seen plenty of noble-born who tromped blithely through spaces and left disaster in their wake. Ádan had a gift for slipping in and making himself just the right shape to fit anywhere.

Korin sat down next to Ádan, facing out towards the cliff and the sky lightening towards dawn.

The silence between them was comfortable and slowly, breath

by breath, Korin's tension drained away. Over the ocean, the sky grew pink, then gold. Morning approaching.

Ádan, too, was looking out over the city, rather than at Korin. Which gave Korin the courage to ask, "Why are you so nice to me?"

Ádan gave Korin a sideways look, curious and thoughtful all at once. "Shouldn't I be?"

"I'm starting to wonder." Korin caught himself fidgeting with his gloves, rubbing the woven material against the scarred skin beneath. "I used to think people were just jumpy around magic. That they didn't understand it, or were superstitious of it. That it was ignorance. But it turns out, maybe they were right and I was wrong. I saw what the Knights could do. I saw…"

Ádan put a hand over Korin's, stilling them. Stilling Korin. "Anyone who's spent more than five minutes with you knows you're not like that."

Ádan's words were no doubt meant to be reassuring, but all they did was reopen that sinking, hollow feeling in Korin's chest. Because what did Ádan know?

Ádan frowned, like he noticed his misstep. He squeezed Korin's hands, then got to his feet, pulling Korin up with him. "Enough of that. Sun's coming up, and we've got somewhere to be."

"We do?"

"Yes. Something you need to do. Something that will make you feel better."

"What's that?" Korin asked, disappointed as Ádan released his hands.

"Someone you can heal."

10

HEY LEFT THE wealthy part of town behind, following the river to the west, beyond any place Korin had yet explored. Here the city sloped down and the ground became soft and marshy. Clouds of flies and mosquitos rose around them. Korin tried ineffectively to wave them away.

"Yeah, the bugs are bad here. This is basically swampland." Ádan slapped at something on his own arm. "But no one around here can afford to ward them off."

The people here were a mix of human and firstborn, and none looked happy to see Korin and Ádan. Because they were strangers? Because of Korin's sigil? Korin's breathing sped, his heart suddenly loud in his ear. "Are we safe here?"

Ádan's eyebrows lifted, like the question surprised him. Then a more thoughtful look crossed his face. "You're safe." He looked Korin straight in the eye. "I promise."

The rush of heat that ran through Korin confirmed that their quiet time on the cliff had done nothing to stabilize his volatile emotions. He had to look away.

A small house—barely more than a shack—set back off the road was where Ádan pointed Korin. "In there. She's expecting us."

Korin knocked and the door opened and then the smell hit. Rotten and wet. The firstborn woman who greeted him was sallow and worn from exhaustion. "Master Wizard. Thank you for coming." She looked over Korin's shoulder at Ádan right behind. "Shaiera's getting worse."

Three single beds covered with netting lined the back wall. Only one was occupied. "I sent the boys away with their dad," the woman said.

Korin wasted no time. He went straight to the little girl huddled shivering and moaning in the bed. He sat down carefully on the edge of the mattress and pulled back the netting. Took a closer look.

Nothing about this was right. The same sickness was inside the girl as had been inside Dustin, as had tried to get into Korin. And Shaiera looked to be in just as much pain as Dustin had been. Maybe more. But that was where the resemblances ended. Dustin's skin had been peeling. This girl's skin was rotting. She had a wet, rattling cough. Dustin had been hot to the touch, but Shaiera was ice cold when Korin felt her forehead.

Dustin had been old, where Shaiera was young. Dustin had been human. Shaiera was firstborn. Were either of these differences enough to justify the startlingly different symptoms? Because on the inside, Shaiera looked exactly the same. That pulsing, hungry darkness consuming her.

More than ever, Korin was convinced there was magic involved.

Korin stroked the girl's cheek. "Shaiera, can you hear me?"

She whimpered, pulled her knees in tighter.

"She hasn't spoken since last night," Shaiera's mother said. "She wasn't this bad. It all came on her so fast."

"How fast?" Korin asked.

"Two days ago she was just fine. Running around, playing with her brothers. Then yesterday afternoon the cough started, but it didn't seem like anything. By yesterday eve, the rash started, and her cough got worse. That was when I went and found Lord Ádan. I'd heard people talking, earlier, that he was looking for people who were sick in a certain way."

In less than a day, this little girl had gone from fine to far worse than Dustin had looked. "It's the blight," Korin said to Ádan. "I'm almost sure of it. Except that it's behaving completely different."

Ádan's expression one of carefully schooled calm. "If I'd known it was this bad, I would have brought you here right away."

"Last night I had no idea she'd get like this," Shaiera's mother was on the edge of tears.

"It's all right," Korin reassured her. "It's going to be all right. Ádan, you know the things I need. Could you go find them for me?"

Horrible as it might sound, Ádan had been right about this making Korin feel better. All his own troubles faded and became inconsequential next to the suffering poor Shaiera was going through. The fact that Korin could help her, could make her well, was better therapy for his own heartache than anything else in the world.

The blight might be hitting her worse than it had Dustin, but it was also hitting her faster, which would work in Korin's favor. He stood up and to Shaiera's mother said, "Help me move the bed around to where I can draw a circle."

Not that the little girl in her bed weighed much of anything, but it gave her mother a way to help. So she didn't have to just stand there and watch her daughter suffer.

Ádan returned with candles and salt and Korin prepared in the same way he had with Dustin. As he lit the candles, he felt the blight inside Shaiera pulse, like it sensed what he was doing. Like it was readying to fight.

Korin smiled. It could fight all it wanted. This time, he was ready.

The magic went much smoother than before. Korin knew what he was doing, knew how to break into the heart of the disease. It didn't have as firm a hold on Shaiera as it had on Dustin. Korin was prepared for when it turned against him and held it away, so all the time it fought him, it was eating into his magic, never into him.

It still took time and patience. Korin was peripherally aware of Ádan standing with Shaiera's mother, offering quiet comfort. Korin was glad to have him there. Even if Ádan couldn't actually do anything to help if Korin ran into trouble, it was nice to have a friend.

Korin drove the blight out of Shaiera, and then spent more time undoing the damage the disease had done. By the time he was finished, Korin was exhausted, but only in the usual way that happened after long, focused magic. He didn't feel consumed, hollowed out by the battle.

Shaiera sat up, rubbing her eyes. Korin waved her mother over and stepped discretely back with Ádan as mother and daughter embraced.

"That looked like it went better," Ádan said, his voice low enough to keep it just between them.

"Much. I'm getting the hang of this thing."

Ádan gave Korin a speculative look that Korin couldn't parse. "What?" Korin asked.

Ádan's lips curved, an almost smile. He reached up to smooth a few stray hairs back from Korin's face, his fingers brushing against Korin's cheek in the process.

Korin couldn't find his next breath.

Ádan's thumb traced the line of Korin's jaw. "You have no idea how..." He trailed off, shook his head. Looked back at Shaiera and her mother, who were still too focused on each other to be paying any attention to Korin and Ádan. Ádan dropped his hand. "Come on, Sunshine. Let's see what these ladies can tell us about what's going on."

. . .

THE ANSWER, it turned out, was not much. They talked to Shaiera, her brothers, and both her parents. None of them could give any clue as to how the girl had gotten sick. She and the boys had been playing, and Shaiera had been out of their sight briefly during that time, but she hadn't gone anyplace strange or disappeared for any unusual length of time. And the boys had no trace of the blight on them.

Like Dustin, Shaiera had no clear memories of the last couple days and had no information to offer.

"I'm glad we were able to help the girl," Ádan said as he and Korin head back into the city, "But I don't feel like we know any more now than we did before."

"We don't." Korin flexed and rolled his fingers, working out the stiffness the magic had brought. The movement drew Ádan's gaze, and Ádan's eyes on Korin's hands brought back the sharp memory of Ádan's fingers on Korin's bare palm. He felt again the ghost touch of Ádan's fingers on his face.

Korin had spent so much of his life hiding. There was no denying Ádan was reaching out, but a part of Korin still couldn't trust enough to reach back.

Korin curled his fingers in again and tried not to think about it. To be safe, he changed the subject. "I'm starving. We pretty much skipped breakfast."

"You've definitely earned some lunch. I know a place, down by the seaport. Amazing fish. We'll eat and we can figure out our next step."

Figure out their next step. Like Ádan's help was a foregone conclusion. Belatedly, it registered what Shaiera's mother had said about Ádan spreading the word, looking for sick people. "Why are you doing this?" Korin asked. "You're going through a lot of trouble to help me. Not that I'm complaining," Korin added quickly.

Ádan waved off the question. "Why not? You're putting more work than I am into helping these people."

"Yes, but this is what I'm trained to do. This is my job."

Ádan flashed him another of those contemplative looks. "According to who? You're a wizard. No one forces you to go out of your way looking for people to heal. Certainly not to do it with asking for anything back. So why would you?"

"Because those people are suffering and I can make it stop. It would be criminal to just ignore them, or turn them away because they have no money."

"Well there you are. If you can help for no reason, then so can I."

Korin was pretty sure Ádan was being purposely evasive. "So you're telling me it's a hobby of yours to pick up random wizards off the street and just throw yourself in with their crusades?"

"You're my first," Ádan admitted. "But it's going well, I think." He winked. "I might just have to make this a habit."

It was a joke, and Korin knew it, and still he felt an irrational stab of jealousy at the thought of Ádan running around with other wizards. "Be serious."

"About what?" Ádan laughed. "What is it you're trying to ask me?"

Why do you like me? Why are you with me? When will you leave? But Korin couldn't ask any of those things. "Don't you have more important things to be doing?"

"Not at the moment," Ádan said with finality. "I'm at your beck and call."

It seemed the best answer Korin was going to get. "All right. Then I call on you to feed me."

Ádan gave a graceful bow without breaking stride. "Your wish is my command."

If only that were true. Because Korin had plenty of wishes.

11

*A*FTER LUNCH, KORIN came home to do more reading. Healing Shaiera had given him another look at the blight, more clues and hints he could hopefully tie to a disease —magical or mundane—that someone else had studied and written about.

He barely noticed the passing of time, until a tap on his shutters pulled him out of a fascinating account of influenza that had spread through Triome a few hundred years ago. That disease had definitely been magic-driven, although this particular journal didn't get into the history of the wizard who had created it or why. And while the flu was nothing like the blight, Korin was learning a lot from the very detailed descriptions of the studies and experiments and eventually treatments this Staff wizard had gone through, picking apart the magical elements from the mundane virus.

More tapping on his shutters. Korin set the book down and went to the window, but the alley outside was empty.

As Korin stepped back, Ádan swung in through the open window, coming down off the roof. "You know, there is a door," Korin said, although he couldn't keep the smile off his face.

"What fun would that be?" Ádan closed the shutters behind him, blocking the sounds of the late evening street.

The room felt suddenly very small. Korin returned to the chair he'd pulled up next to the dresser for a makeshift desk. Ádan sat down on Korin's narrow bed without waiting for an invitation. It made sense—there weren't any other chairs—but Ádan on his bed was distractingly suggestive. And very close. The room was tiny. All Korin would have to do was lean forward and reach out and...

"I've been reading diaries," Korin said, turning his attention back to the books on his desk and *not* to Ádan's long, beautiful fingers spread wide on his sheets. "Other Staff wizards who lived in Triome. Staff and Wing wizards both. I've found some good stuff that may help me figure out easier treatments, but no hint of anything like the blight being seen before."

Ádan scooted back so he could lean against the wall, making himself far too comfortable. "It's magic, right? We know that."

"There's absolutely magic involved, but creating a disease from scratch is hard. And there's no point to it. Nature does a better job of coming up with invasive, scary sickness than we ever could. Magical diseases, they're rare, but when they happen, there's always a base of something familiar to them. Except this one."

Korin pushed the books away from him in frustration. "If there's anything natural about this, it's no disease I've ever seen, or heard of, or read about."

Ádan was listening, nodding along. "Could it be something new? Can that happen? Can diseases just spring into being?"

"Sure. New diseases happen. Old diseases evolve."

Something in his voice made Ádan tilt his head. Out of the corner of Korin's eye, he saw the edge of Ádan's smile. "But you don't think that's what's happening here."

"No. The more I read, the more I actually touch the blight..." All afternoon, Korin's suspicion had been growing. Until he was sure—almost sure. But that didn't make it any easier to say out loud. "I think someone made this. Constructed it. Which is bad enough. And it's unusual. But there's more."

Korin was too aware of the omnipresent sticky heat, of the closeness of the room, of the closeness of Ádan. Handsome, helpful Ádan, whose intelligent brown eyes were locked on Korin, waiting for Korin to continue. Korin felt the warmth of a blush blooming, but a flicker of magic pushed it down before his body could embarrass him.

Focus on the magic, on the blight. Focus on what's important. "The blight—I think it was crafted to kill wizards."

"Wizards like you," Ádan said, the same conclusion Korin had come to.

It thrilled Korin that he hadn't had to spell it out. That Ádan really *was* smart. And brave. Helping Korin solve this problem—contributing. A partner.

Jonathan had never…

But no, Korin didn't want to think about Jonathan.

Ádan, seemingly oblivious to Korin's whirling thoughts, asked the next logical question about the blight. "Who could create something like that? Who would?"

"I don't know." Which was true, sort of.

Ádan didn't let him off the hook. "You have a theory."

The knights were dead, their leaders executed, their order broken. But Korin had seen this same tainted energy in them. And who else would have the means and motive to craft a magical disease that was the most dangerous to the wizards who tried to cure it?

The blight wasn't spreading on its own. So far, it hadn't shown any signs of being contagious. But how far was Korin willing to sink into the realm of paranoid conspiracy to blame these cases on people who were supposed to be long gone from this city?

"Korin?" Ádan's voice, soft, interrupted Korin's thoughts. "You didn't answer."

Because he didn't want to. Because his mind kept skittering

away from the idea that there might still be knights alive. That they might be here, in the city. That they might be hunting wizards like him.

"I need some more time to think."

It was an evasion, but Ádan took it in stride. "Tell me how I can help."

Unbidden came all sorts of ideas of things Ádan could do to help, except they weren't about helping solve the blight at all. Korin had to summon a spark of magic to again keep himself from blushing as his mind conjured images of him on the bed with Ádan, skin against skin, bodies entwined.

Which led to other thoughts, painful and sharp like a sudden slap of cold water. Jon's lips against his, Jon's fingers running through his hair...

Jonathan whose death was Korin's fault. How could Korin sit here and think about...

The touch of Ádan's fingers stroking his palm. Earlier, the way Ádan had traced a finger lightly along his jaw. Had watched him, just like he was doing now, his beautiful eyes locked on Korin's. Like he would never tire of what he saw.

Ádan leaned forward, his elbows resting on his knees, and Korin found himself mirroring the movement. They were so close now, their faces only inches apart.

"Tell me what's wrong," Ádan whispered. "Tell me what's going through your head to make you look so lost."

"I feel lost," Korin whispered back, then shook his head. "No, that's not right. I'm not lost. I'm here. But everyone else—I can't stop thinking about them. Everyone who's gone."

Ádan's hands surrounded Korin's, wrapping them in warmth. "I know what that's like. And I wish I had words to make it better. But I think—I hope—the people we've lost would want their memories to bring us strength. To prop us up rather than dragging us down."

Korin squeezed Ádan's fingers, clinging to them like an anchor.

"It just feels like a betrayal. To be happy. Like I'm forgetting them."

"You're not." Ádan squeezed back, his thumbs stroking, slipping under the edge of Korin's gloves to touch bare skin. "You still get to be happy. You still get to live. The world goes on, and we can miss the people who aren't with us anymore, but we can't stop being who we are."

Korin was hyper-aware of the fact that he and Ádan were alone together. Privacy like he'd never known before. Not as a child, sharing a tiny bedroom with an older brother and younger sister. Not at school, in the cramped underground where all the students were constantly on top of each other. On the road with Teriad, Korin had never had a place that was only his, and he and Jonathan had to steal every moment together.

This was Korin's own room, with a door that closed to keep the world out, and Ádan was no more than a breath away, watching Korin with melting compassion. Light forgive, but Korin wanted this. Wanted…

Korin tilted his head, leaning in just a little more. Ádan moved with him, closing the space between. His lips brushed Korin's, a phantom touch, and Korin sighed.

"You deserve to be happy," Ádan whispered against Korin's lips. "You deserve to have everything you want."

"I don't know what I want." The words were true and not true, spoken without thought. It was hard to will away the guilt, and as much as Korin's body was awake, desperate for Ádan's touch, he couldn't get past this aching feeling of betrayal.

Ádan pulled back, gently. He disentangled one of his hands to lift it to Korin's cheek, cradling Korin's face in a warm touch. "You'll figure it out. And I'll be here when you do." He stood up, sliding his hand down to Korin's shoulder and gave a squeeze. "For now, though, you should probably get some sleep. It's been a long couple days."

It was true. Korin hadn't slept at all last night, which probably had a lot to do with why he couldn't figure out how to work through this. "You're leaving?"

Ádan leaned down and brushed another kiss across Korin's forehead. "I'll see you tomorrow. That's a promise."

He swung out through the window, the same way he'd come in, pulled himself up onto the roof, and was gone.

A GOOD NIGHT's sleep did help. Korin woke refreshed, clear. Things were making sense again.

He was late enough down to breakfast that all the rest of the boarders were gone, so he ate in the kitchen, listening to the girls chatting as they cooked. They talked about family, about plans, about the actor who kept coming around to flirt with Lily, about Verania's sister who had moved north. Korin didn't contribute much, but he felt included and welcome, and that was wonderful.

The afternoon, he spent back in his room, studying, but with much greater focus than before. He no longer felt like he was flailing, but with clarity came a sharper sense of the gaps in his knowledge and a growing conviction of where he needed to go.

Twice, now, he'd been in the academy and both times he'd been driven out. The first time he'd been unprepared and the second time he'd been ambushed. He needed to go back and he needed to make sure he had time to get a solid feel for the place.

These things he knew: the blight that had affected both Dustin and Shaiera had been caused by a person. There was no other explanation. It was contagious, but it had responded to Korin and to his magic with an aggression that a less experienced, less capable healer would not have been able to overcome. It had intent— something no natural or accidental disease could have.

What else Korin knew: that there was some power in the academy that shouldn't be there. It hadn't caused the blight, but it was connected, somehow.

It was getting harder and harder to see any explanation other than that there were still knights alive. That they were here in Triome. The power behind the blight, it wasn't normal magic. It wasn't like anything Korin had ever seen except on the battlefields of Ulek.

The one thing that kept Korin from locking his theory down was that he still hadn't had a chance to get a real sense of the power at the academy. Nikki had interrupted last time. The first time he hadn't known yet what to look for.

So he was almost certain. But all logic implied a tie between the Academy and the blight. Which was why he needed to go there.

This time, Korin made an effort to pay attention as he got close. Especially once he got into the deserted neighborhoods, he stopped and looked around, listened, made certain he wasn't being followed. Making sure no one was around to interrupt him.

In daylight, the academy looked harmless. As before, it seemed to be inviting him in. Korin stood in the entry, but didn't yet step inside. Instead, he closed his eyes, took a deep breath. He sank into himself, focused on his body, listening to his thoughts, reminding himself of *himself*. Who he was, who he wanted to be. Not what this strange place wanted to make him.

Then he stepped inside, opened his eyes, opened himself.

With slow, but deliberate steps, he traversed the grounds. All the while, he listened, trying to reach out with every sense. "I'm here," he murmured. "Talk to me."

As he reached the central courtyard, the whispers started. Low and incomprehensible at first. Korin stopped and waited. He could be patient. "I'm listening," he assured the emptiness. "I want to hear what you need to say."

As before, he felt power move around him. Thick and heavy like a fog rising up from the ground, surrounding him, as the voice resolved into words.

Searching. Lost. Trapped.

Was it talking to him? Or of him? "Can you hear me? Can you talk to me?"

Trapped trapped. Angry. Dead leaves and bits of rot swirled around Korin as a sudden wind rose.

"Who are you?"

Alone. All alone.

Black roots, thick as fingers, erupted from the ground around Korin. They clamped over his feet, wrapped around his ankles. *Stay.*

Korin had been through enough horror that he didn't panic. Instead, he willed a firm *no*, and sent his own magic into the roots, cutting them off from whatever source was guiding them so they fell away.

Had that been an attack? Korin hesitated to call it one, and it had been far less aggressive than the blight. The power here might feel similar, but it was responding in an entirely different way.

Should he understand it? This was the magic of the knights, but also—what Renée had said. His magic. His order. This was what Teriad hadn't wanted them thinking about.

Teriad had been right. Korin wanted nothing to do with this. But if he didn't fix it, who would?

Trapped, the voice had said. Could Korin fix that? What did it even mean?

All this time he'd been looking at diseases that had moved through the city, but he'd never taken a good long look at the Academy itself. At the history. At what had actually happened here.

He needed a history lesson. And who better to help him with that than Ádan?

At that thought, Korin's entire body heated. Korin wanted Ádan. What had seemed so complicated last night had, with sleep, settled into an almost painful awareness of his wanting. Yes, there was still guilt. But there was also need. To feel someone's touch,

their desire—to know he was wanted, to feel safe with someone—
Korin craved that like he needed air.

To not be alone.

That Ádan wanted him too was clear. All he was waiting for
was for Korin to get his head on straight.

Korin made it home and opened the door to his room. Like
magic—like he truly had some innate gift for being exactly where
Korin needed him to be—Ádan was there. Waiting. And with
sudden clarity, Korin knew what he needed to do.

12

*Á*DAN WAS SITTING on his bed, watching Korin with a contemplative smile that had grown painfully familiar in only a few days. A smile that seemed half curiosity, half dare. An undeniable invitation.

Korin wanted Ádan. Had wanted him since the moment Ádan had dragged him out of the haunted academy grounds.

Korin shut the door behind him and took the two steps necessary to cross his small room and stand in front of Ádan. Ádan looked up, still wearing that cryptic smile. He said nothing, but reached out for Korin's right hand. His eyes locked on Korin's, Ádan peeled the glove from Korin's hand and bent forward just enough to place a kiss on Korin's palm.

A spark ran from that point of contact up through Korin's arm, a wave of heat that woke his entire body. Korin pushed Ádan back by the shoulders as he climbed on the bed, on his knees, straddling Ádan's legs. He caught Ádan's mouth in a hungry kiss which Ádan returned with equal urgency.

Safe, this wasn't safe. The thought beat against Korin's mind like a rabbit raising alarm. He pushed it down and away, refused it. Refused to acknowledge it.

The same with the guilt. No thoughts of Jonathan right now. Not if Korin could help it.

Ádan's hands moved down to Korin's hips, dragged him forward and down to grind against Ádan.

Korin's every instinct called out to rush forward, to get through things as fast as possible, before time ran out. Before interruption, discovery. He had to remind himself that this was his room, his space. No one was going to come looking for him. No one was going to question his absence.

Korin pulled back, putting a few necessary inches of space between himself and Ádan. He needed to breathe. Ádan loosened his grip, but didn't let go. He searched Korin's face. "Everything okay?"

Korin didn't know how to answer. He leaned back in, slower this time. He brushed his lips against Ádan's, a whisper of a touch before pressing in tight. Ádan's rough stubble scraped against Korin's chin as Ádan tilted his head to a better angle. Korin ran his tongue over Ádan's lower lip, noting the smooth, soft skin that had probably never been chapped by the cold.

Ádan's hand came up behind Korin's head, fingers tangling in Korin's hair as Ádan held him tight. Ádan worked his other hand in under Korin's shirt and Korin's stomach twitched at the feel of warm skin on skin.

So much heat. From Ádan's body, soaking through the thin clothing between them. The humid weight of the air around them. That had always been another reason to rush—fumbling in the cold, never removing any more clothes than necessary, balancing desire against practicality—a race in the freezing air.

This was pure decadence. "You have no idea," Korin murmured against Ádan's lips, "how different this is from anything I've ever done before."

"I really don't." Ádan separated the width of a breath. "But I'd love for you to tell me."

This question had a safe enough answer that Korin could give it. "There's no rush. No worry someone's going to interrupt us. It's warm; it's comfortable. It feels like we have all the time in the world."

"Time enough," Ádan agreed. He took Korin's hands in his, lacing their fingers together. Without thinking, Korin had kept his hands at his sides, out of the way. Ádan's skin against Korin's one bare hand felt unbelievably intimate. Even more so as Ádan lifted that hand and ran his tongue along the ridges of scar tissue that traced Korin's palm.

"You don't have to do that." Korin heard the waver in his voice. He'd never imagined something could be so exciting and so uncomfortable all at the same time.

Ádan flashed a wicked grin and sucked one of Korin's fingers into his mouth. As if the warm, wet heat against sensitive skin wasn't enough, Ádan's tongue traced the length of Korin's finger, then swirled suggestively around Korin's fingertip.

This was almost more than Korin could take, and they hadn't even removed any clothes.

Korin reluctantly freed his hand from Ádan, then set to work on the buttons of Ádan's shirt. Korin slowly uncovered an expanse of dark skin over sleek muscle that twitched at Korin's slightest touch. Especially once Korin reached Ádan's stomach, where the brush of Korin's fingers made Ádan lean his head back, close his eyes, and sigh.

Korin had never done this with anyone but Jon. In school, he'd been incredibly shy, and had never managed to take advantage of being surrounded by precocious, horny teenagers locked away together through long, dark winters. Still, Korin had listened and Korin had learned, and—above all else—Korin was an expert of anatomy, both human and firstborn.

He leaned forward and traced the outside edge of Ádan's tapered ear with his tongue. Which earned him a groan, and Ádan grabbed him by the hips again and flipped them both around so Korin was on his back and Ádan leaned over him.

"Troublemaker," Ádan murmured as he nipped at Korin's throat, just above the collarbone. At the same time, he pressed down, grinding his hips against Korin's. It felt too good and not good enough. Korin wanted this to last forever and even more he wanted—needed—Ádan to bring him release.

"*Ádan…*" Korin didn't know what more to say. He couldn't make words work in his mind. "Ádan."

Hearing Korin's need, or simply motivated by his own, Ádan kissed Korin deeply as he worked their clothing open enough that there were no barriers between them. All Ádan's teasing manner had gone. They moved together, skin against skin, Ádan's hand around them both. Korin dug his fingers into Ádan's shoulder's, holding on for life. Ádan shuddered against him and the sudden slick, wet heat was enough to push Korin over the edge.

Ádan lay on top of Korin, his face against Korin's shoulder, his breaths slowing to a more normal rhythm. Korin could have lain there forever.

Except that Ádan's knee was digging uncomfortably into Korin's thigh, and they were honestly kind of a mess. "Ádan?"

Korin's whisper against Ádan's ear made Ádan's whole body twitch. He leaned up on his elbows and smiled down and Korin. "Is there something *more* you need?"

Korin looked down at the wrinkled, wet mess of clothing between them, then back up into Ádan's laughing eyes.

"You have a point." Ádan rolled off Korin, landing on his feet with thoughtless grace. Korin sat up, pulled off his shirt and tossed it into the corner, then squirmed out of the rest of his clothes. He felt more than a little self-conscious, fully naked in front of Ádan. This was nothing he'd ever done with anyone, even Jonathan. But Ádan was casually stripping off his own clothes like it was nothing, and Korin hated to choose this moment to seem provincial.

They both made use of the washbasin in a surprisingly comfortable silence. Ádan rinsed his clothes, then spread them over Korin's chair to dry. Korin had no idea what to say or do.

Ádan sat back down on Korin's bed, gloriously, handsomely naked. He really was all muscle, solid and rippling atop his lean firstborn elegance. He tilted his head, gave Korin that familiar, cryptic smile. "You okay?"

"I just...what do we do now?"

"Do you have anyplace you need to be?" Ádan asked.

"No."

Ádan held out a hand. "Then come here."

Korin let himself be pulled down onto his bed. It took some adjusting for them to get comfortable on the bed made for one, but Korin didn't find it at all terrible to be pressed up next to Ádan with nothing else between them. Ádan draped his arm across Korin's chest, stroked Korin's shoulder with his thumb. "Night, Sunshine."

Korin had never in his life slept next to anyone. Certainly not a man with whom he'd just had sex.

Ádan twisted around to lower the cover onto the room's one lamp, then reached down to pull the sheet up over both of them. Korin didn't expect he'd be able to sleep like this, but he'd underestimated his own exhaustion. He was out almost as soon as he closed his eyes.

13

*K*ORIN WOKE FROM his nightmare to a hand on his shoulder and Ádan's voice in his ear. "Easy, Korin. Easy."

Korin's heart pounded; his breath came too fast. He was trapped between the wall and Ádan's body. He pushed up, away, gasping.

Ádan lay where he was. He didn't try to grab Korin or pull him back down. For which Korin was grateful.

The dream was already fading, and with it the panic. "I'm fine. I'll be…I'm fine." As the dream-induced terror faded, guilt crept in. "I'm sorry that I woke you."

Ádan chuckled and slid an arm loosely around Korin's waist. "It's no hardship waking up next to you."

The words, Ádan's hand against Korin's bare stomach, sent a pleasant warmth all through Korin. Even as he blushed, fully awake now and aware of the fact that they were both naked in bed together like a pair of shameless hedonists. That Korin's thigh was pressed against Ádan's awakening erection.

"Lie back down." Now Ádan did tug on Korin, but gently. "You're letting in all the cold air."

"There's cold air here?" Korin lay back, let Ádan pull Korin back against him. Ádan's arms wrapped around Korin's chest and the warm, hard line of Ádan's arousal pressed against the small of Korin's back.

But Ádan seemed content to lie there, his breathing slow and even against Korin's hair. The silence stretched and Korin thought Ádan had fallen back asleep when Ádan asked, "Who's Jonathan?"

Korin tensed. Ádan's palm stroked his chest, soothing. "You don't have to tell me. That's fine. But you said his name while you were asleep." After a pause, Ádan amended to, "While you were in the nightmare."

"He's dead." If Ádan had asked anything, said anything, Korin would have changed the subject. But he lay there, a silent, solid presence. With Korin, but not demanding. Not pushing. Which made it easier—made it *possible* for Korin to talk.

"I told you about Teriad, my teacher, and Lia, his other student. Well, Lia, she had a twin brother. Jonathan." Korin was impressed at how steady he sounded speaking Jonathan's name. "He didn't have anywhere else to go, so Teriad let him travel with us."

Tall and strong, with a dazzling smile that brought something magical to an otherwise plain face. Jonathan had taken instantly to Korin. Treating him first like a brother, and then later...

"Jonathan was like me. Like us." Korin reached back to touch Ádan's thigh, running his hand down the line of smooth skin and hard muscle. "It's dangerous in the south. I don't know what it used to be like, but...it's bad now. Because of..."

"Because of the knights," Ádan finished for him in a soft voice.

Korin nodded and continued. "Jon and I had to hide. And we were always on the road. Never any privacy. We found time together when we could. I loved him. I think. I don't know how you ever really know. I'm pretty sure he loved me. We never said it, because what was the point? It wasn't like we could have a real life."

"You never thought of running off together?" Ádan's question held no accusation. Just curiosity.

"Sure. Sometimes. But I was still learning from Teriad." Korin considered his next words, tested them in his mind to be sure they were true. "The magic was more important. I guess that tells you something. I wanted to be a wizard more than I wanted us to have a life together."

Ádan shrugged, a soft motion against Korin's back. "In my experience, love isn't an all-or-nothing thing. Just because you have a duty to something else doesn't mean you didn't love him. We all have responsibilities. Priorities."

"Except for you," Korin noted. "Who has nothing better to do than pick up random wizards on the street and join in on their dangerous crusades."

"We're not talking about me right now." Something in Ádan's tone sounded off, but that was probably what Korin deserved, trying to joke in the middle of this story.

This story that Korin didn't want to think about. Didn't want to face. But Ádan deserved to hear it. Deserved to know the kind of person he'd taken into bed.

"Ulek went bad at the end. Really bad. The knights were desperate. They'd lost. Everyone knew it. Why they couldn't just surrender…"

The silence stretched, but Ádan said nothing, giving Korin time to find the words.

"We weren't on the front lines at that point. Teriad had settled us in at Naktigan—a trade hub, a little down the mountains. It was where most of the wizard wounded and a lot of the injured soldiers had been assigned. Teriad, Lia, and Jon were asleep. I was on shift in the infirmary."

Korin shook his head. "Infirmary. A bunch of tents all sewn together. It was cold and wet and only a small step up from leaving people lying in the mud. It was exhausting work. None of us had managed a good night's sleep in weeks. We'd all been making mistakes. Teriad—he'd been working through a compli-cated healing—a Wing wizard caught in an explosion. Internal damage. Teriad, he lost focus at the wrong moment. The wizard died."

Ádan's arm tightened around Korin. Korin rested his hand over Ádan's. "It happened. We lost people. Everyone was on edge. Us. The other wizards. But even more, the people. The regular people who'd been caught in this, who had to stand by and watch some of the ugliest, bloodiest fighting in all our history."

Ádan's arm was too constricting. Korin pulled away, sitting up. He leaned back against the wall, his eyes on the other side of the room. Not looking at Ádan.

"I didn't see the ritual. I heard about it, later. How the knights sacrificed their own. Bodies on the ramparts—enough blood to draw a circle around the castle. But I saw the results. That horrible black fog—it reached all the way down to Naktigan. We threw up wards. We didn't know what we were warding against, but if you saw it, you knew you didn't want to be in it. We warded the infir-mary, but the town…

"I saw the people caught out in it. Their bodies just… dissolved. The screams…"

"Shepherd bless," Ádan whispered, a horrified prayer.

"It was the final straw for the townspeople. And I can't…I can't blame them. Magic like that…"

This was the hard part. All Korin could do was push through it. "After the fog cleared, they came with torches. They'd set the place on fire before anyone realized what was happening. It came from nowhere—we were all so tired—no one knew what to do. The tent full of bedding and bandages and alcohol for cleaning wounds—the infirmary went up like a bomb.

"I got out. They were watching for any wizards who escaped."

Korin's voice sounded mechanical to his ears. He felt detached, like he was listening to someone else tell this story. "Five of them with swords and ropes and more torches. They had a noose around

my neck before I could think. I didn't think. I just acted. I…
turned my magic on them. I killed them."

Three words that couldn't begin to encompass the horror Korin
had felt as his magic ripped through them. The sickening knowledge of what he'd done.

"I ran to the barn where we'd been sleeping. Jon was down on
the floor. I told him to run. To meet me outside town. Then I
climbed into the loft for Teriad and Lia. I woke them up and I told
Teriad what had happened. What I'd done."

Korin didn't dare look at Ádan now. If Ádan were wearing that
same look of horror, of disgust, as Teriad had, Korin didn't know
what he would do. "Teriad didn't care about the town. He didn't
care that I'd been attacked. What I did—it went against everything
he believed." *I can't forgive this. I can't teach you anymore.* "He sent
me away. He disowned me."

Naktigan had become a nightmare. Blood and gore in the
streets—the oozing remains of bodies caught in the fog. Suffo-
cating heat and smoke from the fires. The sparking air burning in
Korin's lungs as he tried to navigate out of the town without
drawing attention.

So many bodies. Bodies of wizards who had escaped the
burning buildings only to collapse of smoke inhalation or to be
caught by the mobs. Bodies of townsfolk—like the ones Korin had
left—the ones who had tried to grab wizards or soldiers who were
still capable of fighting back. Or who had been caught in their
own fires.

"Jon wasn't where I'd told him to go. I hadn't thought how bad
it would be, trying to get out. I waited. And then I went back."

Like Korin's worst imagining of Hell, the fires had spread
everywhere. And as if that weren't enough, "There were pyres in
the center of town. They were burning the wizards they'd been able
to capture." A pair of old fortune-teller women with no magic that
Korin had ever seen were among the sacrifices in the square. A
wizard of the Book who had lived in that town all his life. A wizard

of the Sword, his battlefield wounds still fresh enough to be bleeding as his skin turned black.

"Most of the wizards had been in Naktigan because they were too injured to stay on the front lines. Us three Staff Wizards, we were the healers, the only ones able-bodied enough to have a chance. And of the three of us, I was the only one who fought back. Teriad and Lia surrendered. I watched them burn. I couldn't help them. I couldn't save them."

Korin could see the flames, smell the smoke, hear the screams.

"So now you know," Korin finished.

"What happened to Jonathan?" Ádan asked softly.

"I don't know. I never found him. But…everyone saw him with us. With Lia and Teriad and I. They would have…there's no way he could have survived."

Ádan sat up and put a hand on Korin's shoulder. "I'm sorry. Korin, I'm *so* sorry that you had to go through that."

Korin had been so braced for rejection, he froze. His brain couldn't generate a response to sympathy.

Ádan leaned forward, kissed Korin on the forehead, then disentangled himself and got out of bed. "If I could take it all away from you, I could."

He stroked a finger down Korin's cheek. "Try to get some more sleep, Sunshine. The world always looks better in the morning."

Ádan started dressing. "You're leaving?" Korin asked, hoping that didn't sound as pathetic outside his head as within.

"I should go. It's late. Early," he corrected himself with a grin, but something was off about his smile.

Korin wanted to tell him not to go. To beg him to stay. But something in the air between them had changed. Korin had changed it. Better to let Ádan go.

With a final wave, Ádan climbed back out the window and pulled himself onto the roof. Korin lay back down, unhappy and lonely in a way he hadn't been since he'd arrived in Triome.

One small blessing. He had no more nightmares for the rest of the night.

FIRST THING IN THE MORNING, Korin went to Renée's to offer her a delayed apology.

Renée was in her shop, and greeted Korin cheerfully, although she didn't look up from her microscope to do so. "Come give me a hand."

Korin dutifully took a seat across the counter from her and used his magic to steady the circuit board on which Renée was manipulating wires too small for Korin to see. It was something Korin had plenty of practice with after seven years at the Crystal. "What are you building?" he asked.

"Nothing yet. I'm still experimenting." Her hands were cupped around the board, fingers twitching as she used her own magic to manipulate the wires with finer control than any hand-held tool could give. "Just read Perry's latest paper on electromagnetic fields, and I'm pretty sure he's got something wrong, but I can't dig out his mistake till I've got a—steady, Korin! Till I can replicate his process."

She sat up and Korin felt the air around them both ease as she released her magic. "Only so much of that I can do at a time." She rubbed her eyes, then looked Korin up and down. "And how are you today?"

So much had happened since he'd dragged her out of bed in the middle of the night. What could he even say? "I don't know."

"Hmm." Renée leaned back in her chair, crossed her arms. "All right then. Tell me what more you've learned about the blight."

This was safer ground. Korin told her about healing Shaiera, about the reading he'd done. He talked about the way the blight fought him, the ways it had changed and the ways it hadn't. Renée heard what he was saying, and possibly what he wasn't, and said, "You think someone made this. You think it's a weapon."

"It's worse than that." He told her about the academy, about his suspicion there were still knights around. Whether it was time or repetition or just the release of tension that last night with Ádan had been, Korin was able to say the words without his heart racing or the feeling he couldn't breathe. "And I don't know what to do," Korin concluded.

Renée tapped her fingers on the counter. Careful, even as her mind was elsewhere, not to disturb her project. "Normally I'd say go talk to your Archwizard. Except I've met your Archwizard. Man's a menace. No offense. If some rogue wizards—or, Light forbid, more knights—are involved in magical fuckery, I can't imagine he'd care. Less it was getting in the way of his own magical fuckery."

"*Renée.*"

"Don't scold your elders, Korin. Let me think." Her fingers continued to drum, until she shook her head. "This is way outside my expertise. Maybe if you had tangible evidence—another victim, perhaps—you could take it to the Council of Nine, but frankly, after all that nonsense down in Ulek, the council isn't eager to stir up any trouble. They're going to be cautious. It's been a big, public thing that the knights are gone. If that turns out not to be true, that could come down hard on the orders. And after all that corruption, I don't know if it would be better or worse if it turns out it's not more knights. That it's just wizards abusing their power."

"But that doesn't even make any sense. If the council won't protect people from magic being used badly—it's…it's irresponsible!" Korin was offended by the very idea.

"That's life. Full of lazy asses in power just trying to do the least possible work it takes to get by."

"We have an obligation." Korin was quoting Teriad now, and it hurt a little. "We have the power to help people, and it's our job to use it. To leave the world better than we found it. If there's something that only I can do, then it's my responsibility to see it done." He slowed down at Renée's bemused expression. "Isn't that right?"

"Oh kid, there are no easy answers. The world's complicated, and I wish it were as easy as you say." She sighed and rolled her shoulders, preparing to settle back in at the microscope. "But you're not a fool, and I think you know as well as I do that it isn't."

Korin didn't know how to respond to that. So he put his hands back in place to help her with the board. "Ready when you are."

Renée leaned in and that was the end of talk of the blight for the morning.

14

*A*ROUND LUNCHTIME, KORIN returned to Marta's. Lily's brother was there with a shoulder he'd injured years ago that had never healed quite right. It was just the challenge Korin needed after a morning of mindless, repetitive assistance to Renée. While Korin worked, the girls moved in and out of the kitchen, doing the afternoon cleaning and starting on dinner, chatting with each other, with Lily's brother, with Korin. Marta came through, told Korin to make sure he wasn't in the way with her usual brusqueness, but also set a paper-wrapped bundle down on the table next to him. One that turned out to have a flaky guava pastry in it.

It felt a lot like a home.

After Korin had fixed the shoulder—an impressive bit of magic given how long the injury had been there, not that Korin could say so—Lily's brother told him about a fever and cough moving its way through the kids in his neighborhood. So Korin followed him home to scout out the problem.

Nothing serious, thank the Light. Korin triaged the worst cases and gave out a recipe for an herbal tincture that would help with the coughs. He promised to come back over the next few days to help with any more who fell ill and follow up on the rest.

It was getting dark. The end of an altogether productive day. What Korin might have called a great day, except for one tiny detail.

No Ádan.

Korin had the entire day to second guess his middle-of-the-night confession. The longer he went without Ádan materializing out of nowhere with a wink and a grin, the more Korin started to think he'd made a mistake. The conversation, certainly. The sex… maybe.

Doubts and second thoughts. Probably irrational. Definitely premature. But knowing that didn't stop Korin from obsessing. Had he said the wrong thing? Done the wrong thing? Had he disappointed Ádan? Scared him away?

Was it too pathetic for words to go looking for Ádan?

Activity at Marta's was starting to pick up for the evening, so no one noticed when Korin slipped back out. He didn't have a solid idea of where to go if he wanted to find Ádan.

Come to think of it, he had no idea where Ádan lived, where he spent his time, anything. What *did* Korin know about him? Ádan had effortlessly inserted himself into Korin's life. He knew the friends and habits Korin had developed in Triome. But Ádan had shared…nothing.

All Korin could do was retrace the paths they'd wandered together. The restaurant near the docks. The marketplace. The sun sank below the horizon as he walked by the school, by Renée's. And finally, for lack of any better idea, Korin turned towards the academy.

Which turned out to be the right choice. Before Korin had made it too far into the abandoned streets of this ruined part of town, he heard Ádan's voice ahead. But Ádan wasn't alone.

"…of all people should know better," Nikki's voice was clear in the evening air. "It's dangerous."

Ádan's response was lower, but Korin could still hear him. "I know. *I know.* I made a mistake. How was I supposed to guess—"

"We can't afford mistakes. Prophet's balls, Ádan. I can't believe you had sex with him."

Korin's face burned hot. They were talking about him.

"He's using you," Nikki went on.

"He's not like that."

Even in his hurt, his confusion, Korin felt a pang of happiness at how quickly and adamantly Ádan had spoken in his defense.

"You don't know anything about him. And every time we turn around, he's poking at the Academy. He's a Staff wizard. He was *in Ulek.*"

"But he's also...you don't know him, Nikki. He cares so much for people. He bleeds for them. I don't think he has it in him to use anyone. He's the kindest, sweetest... I really like him."

Korin's skin burned and his ears rang at the intensity of Ádan's words.

"He seemed so perfect," Ádan continued, his voice heavy with defeat. "Like he could have...but you're right. I can't. Not after what he's been through. If he hadn't been in Ulek. If he weren't so..."

Korin didn't want to hear the rest. He turned to go back the way he'd come, but his foot scraped the ground. The noise was too loud in the empty street. The conversation stopped. Korin froze. He heard footsteps moving away, fading into silence, and then Ádan came around the corner of the building just ahead. He stopped as he saw, "Korin?"

"I heard you," Korin said in a surprisingly calm voice. "You and Nikki. I heard what you said. About me being a mistake."

Ádan pushed his hand back through his thick dark hair, looking frustrated and dispirited and nothing like his usual buoyant self. "Korin, I'm sorry. It's complicated and unfair and look, you have to know that—"

"What? What do I have to know?"

Ádan didn't answer. They stood in uncomfortable silence, staring at each other.

Until a deep, raspy voice from the shadows behind Ádan said, "Grab the wizard. Kill the other one."

Ádan whipped around and had his sword out before Korin could think. Two shapes in the darkness in front of them, and the sound of another behind. Adrenaline shot through Korin as his mind stuttered to a halt.

Ádan pushed Korin to the side, so Ádan was between Korin and all three attackers. But he was one lone man with a sword against three hulking brutes who were after a wizard.

They needed to see. That was easy magic that didn't require thought. Korin threw up his hand and shot a burst of energy into the air. White light filled the street. Korin got a good look at his attackers. And for the second time in as many minutes his mind froze.

They were men—probably. Too tall, too broad, disproportioned and lumbering. Like they'd been inflated from the inside, only their skin hadn't all stretched out the same way. It was cracked, oozing. All three were missing fingers. One had lost an entire hand. One had his mouth open and his tongue was obviously gone. The other two were lacking an ear each.

"*Light.*" Korin stumbled. He blinked and looked again with wizard sight. These men—these creatures—were full of the writhing energy of the blight.

Ádan recovered from the sight faster than Korin. He jumped at the closest attacker, his sword a blur. These men were big and slow. Ádan's sword sank deep into the man's neck in what was obviously a killing blow. Ádan spun to face the next.

The giant that should have been dead grabbed Ádan's arm. Stopped him short.

Korin acted without thinking. He reached out towards the giant, reached with his magic. Just as before, in Naktigan, he struck to kill. Sent his power deep inside the man to rip him open from the inside.

Nothing happened.

Ádan had a knife in his other hand, stabbed it hard into the monster's chest. Right through his heart.

Nothing happened.

No blood. No sign the giant had felt any pain.

The monster lifted Ádan by his arm and threw him against the nearest building with enough force to crack the plaster wall.

"Ádan!"

The other two monsters advanced on Korin. He aimed his magic like a spear, a piercing beam of pure energy. Dangerous, uncontrolled, it should have burned them to dust.

No purchase. The power sank into them and fizzled into nothing. Couldn't touch them or the corruption inside.

The ground broke at Korin's feet, rising up. A wall of earth and stone, tall and thick, blocking Korin from the monsters. Ádan grabbed Korin's arm. "Run!"

Another finger of stone reached up from the ground, pushed back at the giant that had thrown Ádan. Magic. Korin whipped his head around to find the other wizard.

But there was no wizard. There was only Ádan. Ádan pushing his hand through the air to send the stone wall rippling like a wave.

Ádan using magic.

Ádan could do magic.

Korin yanked his arm free of Ádan's grip. Everything snapped together. Ádan at the academy. Ádan's evasiveness. Ádan's interest in the blight. Korin's suspicions and growing conviction. "There *are* some left. You're one of them! You're a—"

"Yes!" Ádan grabbed Korin's arm again and pulled. "You can hate me later. Come *on*!"

As one of the monsters shattered the stone wall with a massive, swollen fist.

Korin ran.

THROUGH THE DARK STREETS, they ran. Ádan cut through crumbling courtyards and tight alleys. The monsters followed behind. Slower, but untiring and implacable. Korin fed his body energy to keep going, but he couldn't keep from stumbling over uneven ground in the dark.

Korin had no idea how long they ran before Ádan turned sharply and pulled Korin into an open building. He pushed Korin back against the wall and pressed against him in the darkness. "Shhh," he whispered in Korin's ear. "Don't move."

Korin did his best. His gasping breaths were too loud, and he couldn't suck in enough air to make them stop. His chest heaved against the warm weight of Ádan's body.

This time, he felt the magic as Ádan cast it. A shiver in the air that deepened the shadows around them and dulled the sounds from outside.

The monsters lumbered by the crumbling house in which Korin and Ádan stood hidden. They didn't turn, didn't look. Kept going into the night.

Neither Korin nor Ádan moved for quite some time. Korin was aware of his heart pounding. Of the heat coming off Ádan. Ádan's hand pressed against the wall next to Korin's ear. Ádan's rough breathing that stirred Korin's hair.

Korin had used his magic like a weapon again. It had come easy, reflexively. Even though it hadn't worked, the very fact of it made him sick inside. Korin put his hand on Ádan's chest and pushed him away. "I think they're gone."

Ádan took a couple steps back, visibly flinching when he put weight on his right foot. Considering the force with which he'd been thrown against a building, he was probably lucky he could walk at all. "What were those things?" Ádan muttered, easing his head around the corner to look up and down the street.

That should have been Korin's biggest concern. What they were. Who they were. Why they were after Korin. Or he could focus on the churning in his gut at how quick and easy it was for him to toss his every moral code to the side. But all he could think about was, "You're a knight."

"I am." Ádan turned back to face Korin. Not that Korin could see anything but the vague shape of him in the darkness. "And we should probably talk about that, but not in the street. Especially not with those things still out there."

"You lied to me."

"Yes." It was something that Ádan didn't try to deny it. "Now are you coming?"

Korin couldn't argue with the need to get off the street. "Where?"

"Someplace safe. Someplace these things shouldn't be able to follow."

Korin nodded. Realized Ádan probably couldn't see the movement. Said, "Okay."

This time they moved slower through the street. Ádan led cautiously, noticeably limping. After a couple blocks, Korin couldn't stand it. "Wait," he said softly.

Ádan looked around alert for danger. "What is it?"

"Nothing. Hold still."

Ádan froze as Korin lay his hands on Ádan's hip and thigh. The fresh injuries were easy to find and easier to heal. Korin knitted muscle, eased bruises, and erased the web of fractures that marked where Ádan had struck the wall. "Okay?"

Ádan caught Korin's hands. "Korin…"

Korin pulled away. "Keep moving."

With his body back in fully working order, Ádan moved like a shadow. Silent and swift through the dark, abandoned streets. Korin's own footsteps sounded too loud and echoey, the decaying stone beneath his feet both crunchy and slippery. And all the while, as he tried and failed to ghost along like Ádan, Korin's every nerve was on alert for the sound of the monsters returning.

Korin was working so hard at being quiet, he didn't notice where they were going. Not until the crumbling archway that led to the academy was before him. "What are you—"

Ádan cut him off with a sharp gesture, knifing his hand through the air. He pointed ahead, at a decaying mansion that sat with its back to the academy wall. If this was Ádan's idea of safe…

After one final careful look all around, Ádan climbed in through one of the wide ground-floor windows, its glass long gone. Korin followed. Ádan stayed at the window, unmoving, watching out. Korin waited, hidden behind the wall. Given the deeper darkness inside the house, no one from the street would be able to see Ádan. Korin knew he was there and could barely pick Ádan's shape out from the shadows.

Ádan in his midnight blues, grays, and blacks, clothes that blended into the darkness like he was part of it. In this city of bright colors and brighter sun, Ádan dressed for exactly what he was doing now. How had Korin never noticed that?

After an indeterminate amount of waiting, Ádan waved for Korin to follow him deeper into the decaying house. Between delicate marble columns that surrounded what had once been a sprawling, open dining room. Through an inner courtyard that had grown into its own micro-jungle. Up a wide, spiraling staircase that pitched to one side and looked ready to fall at any moment. Into an upstairs bedroom, where Ádan led them into a closet the size of Korin's room at Marta's.

On the back wall, Ádan sketched a glyph, his fingers leaving glowing traces of the lines as he drew them. The wall before him dissolved, opening into a dark staircase leading down. "Go ahead," Ádan whispered. "Once I've closed the door behind us, we can have light."

Once revealed, the secret passage—for what else could it be?— was in much better shape than the rest of the house. No rot in the wood. Fresh paint. And fresh magelights along the walls that Ádan called awake with a wave of his hand.

Korin counted the steps as they descended. One flight down, then two, then three. Deep below the city streets before they reached the next door that Ádan opened with another magic glyph.

Korin walked into an underground palace. A mix of firelight and magelight danced and reflected off multicolored glass and burnished gold. Fake stained glass windows with bright light behind created the illusion of openness, and the mosaicked ceiling and walls erased any hint of being in a cave. The furniture, the lamps, the fireplaces, all ornate and lush, rich fabric and polished wood, and layered in more gold than Korin had ever seen in his life.

Korin knew—everyone knew—that the knights had money. They'd had kings and princes among their ranks. Before their disgrace, they'd been the first choice of profession for noble sons and daughters who showed any leaning towards magic. Korin had heard plenty of speculation that their immense wealth had contributed to their downfall. Although Korin had never heard those words from anyone with magic of their own. There were greater temptations in the world than anything a few coins could buy.

"This is where you live?" Korin asked, overwhelmed by the opulence.

"It's a safe house."

Korin didn't miss the way Ádan hadn't answered his question. "Am I allowed to be here?"

Once again, Ádan evaded. "Come on. We should talk to Nikki and V sooner rather than later."

"No." Korin planted his feet. "We have to talk about this. You and I. I want to know what you've dragged me into."

"What do you want me to say?" Ádan asked. "Would it help if I apologize? Because I can. I *do*. I'm sorry for everything that's happened. There's a lot I would have done differently. But…we're here now. And we're just going to have to move forward."

Ádan was sorry. Korin turned away, his fists clenched, his chest too tight to continue. Ádan had lied. Ádan would have done it all differently. Being with Korin was a mistake. "How could you even…how could you be one of *them*?"

Ádan's hands were a warm weight on Korin's shoulders. "I'm truly sorry."

Korin had fought his way through the recent weeks and months by dividing the world into black and white, into good guys and bad guys. People to blame for the horrors he'd seen versus the people who were victims. He wasn't ready for the world to be more complicated. A more complicated world could break him wide open.

But he'd managed this far by simply willing himself to keep going. "I need to understand what's going on."

"Just bear with me a little longer. Once we're settled in, once I know we're safe, I'll answer your questions."

What choice did Korin have?

15

HE SAFE HOUSE—or was it safe cave?—was huge in comparison to the mansion over their heads, larger and far more luxurious than any house that Korin had ever seen or stayed in back in the south. But it felt immediately comfortable for Korin. The Crystal hadn't been near this ornate, and most of its space had been cluttered with experiments and piles of books and the occasional napping student, but underground had the echoes of home for Korin. It felt safe.

At least until Ádan led him into the little kitchen area, where Nikki and another firstborn sat across from each other, playing stones. The two looked up. Nikki slammed a hand down on the table, making the little black and white pieces jump and scatter. "What the *hell*, Ádan?"

His voice utterly calm, Ádan said, "Korin of the Staff, allow me to introduce Cavaliers Nikhil and Varajas, both formerly of the Sunburst. Both fellow Knights."

Varajas looked a little older than Ádan, not that it was ever easy to guess the age of a firstborn. His copper skin and smooth black hair marked him as probably local. He looked Korin up and down, calmly assessing, then turned his attention to putting the game board back to rights. "I see we've already given up on our secret identities?"

"I have my reasons for bringing him here," Ádan said.

"I should think."

Nikki glared, first at Ádan, then at Varajas. "Is that all you're going to say?" he demanded.

Varajas shrugged. "It's done. I'm sure Ádan thought he was doing the right thing. And with both Kolyn and Derian dead, there's no one to say he's wrong."

"*I'll* say it. I already said it. And not half an hour ago, you agreed with me, Ádan."

Ádan leveled a cool glare back at Nikki. "The situation's changed."

Watching this little drama play out might have been more interesting if Korin hadn't been at the center of it. "I didn't ask to be brought here."

"None of us did," Nikki snapped.

"Light's sake, Nikki, could you just calm down?" Varajas leaned back in his chair and studied Korin with all the warmth of a snake considering its next meal. "I'm sure Ádan's going to enlighten us on why he thought it so important he bring a guest to dinner."

"Yes. It's time we all had a talk." Ádan took a seat at the table. Korin, after a moment's hesitation, took the remaining empty chair, which put him between Varajas and the still-seething Nikki.

"So there's the blight," Ádan said. "Korin's name for it is as good as any. You know about the people Korin's been healing, but tonight we saw something new.

"I don't even know how to describe them. People, I guess, but huge. It was like..." he trailed off, obviously struggling to find the words.

Despite himself, Korin stepped in to help. "They were out of proportion. Like parts of them had grown faster than others. Their skin—I don't know if you saw this—but it cracked open in places. Like it had burst. Like they'd grown so fast it couldn't keep up. And all through them, with my wizard sight, I saw the blight."

Ádan nodded. "I hurt two of them. Injuries that should have been fatal, and they shrugged it off like it was nothing. Didn't even bleed."

"Well this is somewhat alarming," Varajas said, tapping his chin thoughtfully.

"Why?" Korin's question got all three knights looking at him. "You're all acting surprised, but isn't this your magic? I saw the blight, or its close cousin, long before I got to Triome. I saw it in knights."

"Well done," Nikki sneered at Ádan. "What secret are you going to share next?"

"Nikki, would you please shut up?" Varajas asked in a pleasant tone.

Korin was about done. "If someone doesn't start talking *to* me —if you don't start telling me the truth—I'm leaving."

Varajas leaned his elbows on the table, resting his chin on his fist. "You're going to tell him, aren't you?" he asked of Ádan.

"What choice do we have? Seriously, Nikki, V. I have a duty here. And I only see one way forward to fulfill it."

Nikki shook his head. "We don't know they're all dead. If we just wait, there could be others trying to get here. We can't be the only ones—" Abruptly he stood, knocking the table back as he did so. "Fuck you, Ádan. And you, too," he said to Korin. "Do whatever you want. You always have."

Nikki stormed out—there was no other way to describe it. Varajas sighed. "I'll go talk to him." He stood, more relaxed than Nikki had been. "Do you want my opinion?"

"Of course," Ádan said. "Yours and Nikki's both."

"Your instincts have always been good, Ádan. There's a reason the Grandmaster chose you for this. Just be careful you're rebuilding for the right reasons." With that, Varajas left Korin and Ádan alone together.

In the silence that followed, Ádan looked across the table at Korin. Korin looked across the table at Ádan. Not twenty-four hours ago they'd been pressed together, as close as two people could get, and now it felt like a gulf of a thousand miles separated them. Impossible that it was only the width of a table.

"I'm sorry," Ádan said.

"You've said that already."

"I mean it."

Another long silence passed between them. Korin wasn't sure what the worst part about all of this was. That Ádan had lied to him. That Ádan was a knight.

Or that Korin still, despite everything, wanted him.

"Were you planning to just disappear?" The question came unbidden to Korin's lips. "Sleep with me and then never see me again?"

"Yes." Ádan didn't even have the good grace to look ashamed. "If I'd known what you went through—what you went through because of us—and I should have. I should have asked before. I knew you were angry with the knights. I just had no idea…"

He put his hand out, like he was reaching for Korin, then caught himself and pulled back. "The trouble, Korin, is that I like you. I like you a lot. You help people without even thinking about it. You're kind in ways I'd forgotten people could be. You're sincere, you're honest. You're talented. I don't think you even know how gifted a wizard you are. And you're beautiful."

Korin took a sharp breath and had to look away. Yesterday, he would have given anything to hear these words from Ádan. Today —now—he'd lost all sense of how to deal with this.

And Ádan wasn't done. "You're perfect. Everything I could have asked for. Until you told me you were in Naktigan. That because of us, you lost your teacher and your friend and your lover. And I realized I couldn't do it. I couldn't ask you to…"

"To what?" Korin prompted when Ádan trailed off.

Ádan sighed. "To help us." He reached out again, and this time he didn't stop himself. His hand slid across the table to find Korin's, as he caught Korin's gaze and held it. "To save us."

Korin jerked his hand away, hating himself for the thrill that still ran through him at Ádan's touch. "Why should I want to save you?" Did the words sound as false to Ádan as they did to Korin?

Or did he take them at face value? "I understand. I do. It's a fair answer, and I can't blame you for it."

"So what now?" Korin asked.

Ádan looked up, frowning. "I don't know how safe it is for you to leave. Whatever those monsters were—I'd feel better if we all stayed hidden till morning. There's plenty of room here. The three of us will leave you alone. I promise."

Korin didn't care for the idea of overnighting here, but he recognized the sense of Ádan's suggestion. It wasn't worth the risk of running into those creatures again. Especially if he was on his own. "All right. I'll stay."

"Excellent." Ádan leaned back in his chair, flashed Korin a smile. A pose, Korin was almost certain. "Come on, Sunshine. I'll find you a room."

ÁDAN ESCORTED KORIN TO A LONG, narrow room that held a half dozen two-tiered bunk beds. "No one will bother you in here. If you get hungry or anything, there's food in the pantry. Make yourself at home." His tone was light, like Korin was a guest who'd just dropped in for an overnight. Korin found himself wondering just how good an actor Ádan might be.

He'd fooled Korin. Misled him. Distracted him. Korin could look back now at Ádan's interest in the blight, at both his and Nikki's presence around the Academy, as obvious clues of their real identity. But Korin had let himself be taken in by Ádan's charm and flattery, had never asked the questions he should have.

Ádan withdrew, leaving Korin alone. He sat down on one of the beds, but there was no way he was going to sleep any time soon.

Alone in the quiet, Korin couldn't stop himself from endlessly rehashing the last couple days. His night with Ádan. That disastrous talk. Those monsters in the street.

Ádan was a knight. Ádan was a knight.

Ádan was a knight.

Korin stood back up. He needed to move, and this narrow, cramped room was too small. Ádan had told Korin to make himself at home, so he couldn't object to Korin wandering.

The underground safehouse had obviously been designed to support a large number of knights. There were three kitchens—the one Korin had been in, another like it on the opposite end of the hall, and a much larger space that could probably provide food for hundreds. Alongside the sitting area Korin had come through on his way in, the front halls connected to a gymnasium, another room with mats on the floor and weapons on the wall, and a magical workroom with circles inscribed on the floor and symbols painted on the walls.

More bunk rooms like Korin's. Enough beds to sleep a hundred and fifty people. A few smaller, nicer bedrooms that had obviously been meant for officers or nobles. Three of these, the doors were closed. Korin assumed those rooms had been claimed by Nikhil, Varajas, and Ádan.

Further on, a stone staircase led down. Curious, Korin followed it. The cool, dry underground air changed as he descended, becoming warmer and wetter, with just a hint of sulfur. Korin recognized that smell, and knew what it meant. Somewhere close the knights had an underground hot spring.

The hot pools had been one of the best parts of the school of the Crystal—natural springs expanded with magic and engineering into one of the central gathering spots for everyone who lived there. It had been Korin's favorite place to escape the cold, and while he'd left the cold far behind, the pure, sensual joy of soaking in the hot water was still every bit as tantalizing.

The door to the pools was half-open. Korin looked in on a cavern that seemed almost as large as the entirety of the space above. Water bubbled and steamed in a large central pool and was diverted off to smaller basins with benches carved into their stone walls, then continued on to the small stream through which it drained out under the far wall. The air was thick and steamy and soaked into Korin's skin.

Awed by the room, it wasn't till Korin took a second look that he realized he wasn't alone.

Ádan lay in one of the smaller pools. He half-floated, with his head tilted back against the edge and his eyes closed. He hadn't noticed Korin. Korin could back away quietly and Ádan would never know he'd been here.

Korin didn't move. He couldn't look away. Ádan relaxed was Ádan at his most handsome. The tense, anxious thoughts that had been whirling through Korin's head broke apart. In their place, just as unbidden, memories of Ádan's touch. Ádan's smile. The brush of Ádan's fingers against Korin's cheek. Ádan's laugh.

In the morning, Korin would leave and never look back. He wanted nothing to do with the knights. After everything they'd done, all the people they'd killed, all the horrors they'd visited upon the world, the best thing Korin could do was to walk away.

But that was tomorrow. Tonight...

Was it so wrong to want one more night?

Assuming Ádan wanted that too. What did Korin know about what Ádan wanted? Ádan had said his time with Korin was a mistake, but what did he really mean by that.

Korin wanted to know. Korin needed to know. Even if, after tonight, he never saw Ádan again.

"Ádan."

Ádan's eyes fluttered open and he lifted his head. "Korin?" The uncertainty in his tone—it was the first time Korin had heard Ádan sound anything but sure of himself. It decided Korin.

"Do you mind if I join you?"

The slow smile that spread across Ádan's face was an undeniable invitation.

16

ORIN WALKED OVER to the pool. He only realized after he got there that Ádan was utterly naked. It hadn't occurred to Korin Ádan might be. The baths at school hadn't been like that. They were public; people had always worn bathing clothes of some sort.

Ádan didn't seem at all uncomfortable having Korin there, looking at him. Wasn't this what Korin had hoped it would come to?

Ádan still hadn't said anything. He studied Korin, and somehow Korin felt like he was the naked one. Needing to break the too-intimate silence, he blurted the first words he could think of. "I seem to be overdressed."

Ádan stood slowly, then put his hands on the side and levered himself up out of the pool. The muscles along his shoulders and down his back flexed with the easy motion. In two steps he was standing in front of Korin. In a low voice, he said, "I could help with that."

Korin nodded his assent. Ádan slid his hands up under Korin's shirt. Ádan's skin was overwarm and rough from the water. He left a damp trail up Korin's stomach, over his chest, scraping Korin's nipples with his thumbs as he went. Korin's body cared nothing for the doubts and hesitations swirling through Korin's mind. It only knew the heat of the room, the heat of Ádan's touch. Korin was hard and ready and it was already impossibly difficult to remember why he'd hesitated at all.

Ádan lifted the loose shirt over Korin's head, slid it down Korin's back, freed Korin's arms, then tossed it aside. Korin kicked off his shoes as Ádan's hands ran down his sides, skimmed over his hips—first outside his clothes, then again, burrowing under to bare skin.

Leaning forward, Ádan slowly closed the distance between them to catch Korin in a languid kiss. His tongue probed Korin's mouth as his thumbs ran along the top edge of Korin's thigh and his fingertips dug into Korin's ass. Korin stopped thinking, stopped worrying, let his thoughts melt into his body.

Ádan sucked in Korin's lower lip, worried it gently, then moved down to Korin's neck, his lips and teeth finding sensitive spots Korin hadn't known existed. Korin had to put his hands on Ádan's shoulders to steady himself as Ádan sank lower, kissing his way down Korin's chest as he pushed the rest of Korin's clothes down. Ádan ended up on his knees before Korin, but stopped his progress with a kiss just below Korin's navel. He reached up to Korin's hands on his shoulders, brought them to his mouth, peeled off Korin's gloves and sucked on each fingertip in turn. The feel of Ádan's tongue against Korin's rough, scarred skin was dangerously intimate and desperately erotic all at once. Korin swayed forward, as Ádan pulled back.

Ádan looked up at Korin, a teasing smile dancing across his lips. "Ready for the pool?"

At this moment, Korin would have agreed to anything. He stepped free of the puddle of clothes at his feet and let Ádan pull him over to the water.

The silky heat of the water sliding over his skin was as amazing as Korin remembered from school. This was even better. With no clothes, it enveloped him, embraced him.

"The look on your face right now," Ádan whispered against Korin's ear. His tongue traced along Korin's earlobe, making Korin twitch. "I start to think beneath that controlled wizard veneer lurks a true sensualist."

Korin turned in Ádan's arms, done with games, done with slow. He straddled Ádan's lap, feeling his every movement against the water, a constant caress along his awakened, sensitized skin. Ádan's fingers dug into Korin's shoulders as Korin caught his mouth in a hungry, desperate kiss. Ádan's tongue swirled around his own as their bodies pressed together.

Ádan's hands moved down Korin's back, a relaxed, indolent stroke, but Korin could feel the tension in Ádan's body. It echoed the need in his own. The water made a delicious, slippery friction between them.

Korin rubbed against Ádan, lost in the sensation. Till Ádan caught his hand again and leaned back to put space between them. With unquestionable deliberation, Ádan moved Korin's hand down to wrap it around Ádan's cock.

Korin froze.

"Korin?" Ádan asked.

"I'm sorry. I just didn't think…" The words sounded stupid as they came out of his mouth. "Jon never wanted me to…because of my scars…"

Ádan's raised eyebrow communicated a world of disdain, but the look was erased with a blissful sigh, as Korin wrapped his fingers tighter. Korin stroked slowly up and down, getting to know Ádan's shape, the feel of his skin, the weight of him in Korin's hand.

Ádan closed his eyes, leaned his head back. "There you go, Sunshine. Just like that."

Korin kept going just like that. Until Ádan's hands clutched at Korin's hips and his body tensed. Korin took that cue to speed up and Ádan's hips bucked against Korin's hand. Ádan's whole body tensed as he climaxed. Korin continued to stroke until the twitch of Ádan's hips told him to stop.

As Ádan reclined, recovering, Korin couldn't resist running his hands over Ádan's chest. Feeling the hard muscles under Ádan's dark skin. Moving lower, Korin ghosted his fingertips over Ádan's stomach. Ádan flinched, caught his wrists. "Too much," he said, but with a smile to take away any sting. Then, "Your turn."

Ádan turned them both around and before Korin knew what he was doing, Ádan had lifted him by his hips up onto the edge of the pool. The air was sudden coolness against his skin and Korin was about to protest just as the wet heat of Ádan's mouth descended on his cock.

Korin buried his fingers in Ádan's hair and thrust into Ádan's mouth. He wrapped his legs around Ádan's back, lost in the delicious heat and pressure of Ádan's lips and tongue. This was unlike anything Korin had ever experienced. Every rushed, frantic, half-freezing encounter with Jonathan might as well have been a different act.

This was lingering and sultry. Ádan's hands traced heated lines up his thighs and over his hips. His mouth was warm, soft. His tongue, velvet. All Korin could do was surrender to the pleasure building inside him as Ádan expertly coaxed him to orgasm.

Ádan's throat worked as he swallowed, then gently released Korin. With a self-satisfied smile, he pulled Korin back into the water.

Korin never wanted to move again. He closed his eyes as Ádan settled them both on the pool's bench, wrapping his arms around Korin's chest and one leg over Korin's thighs, holding Korin against him.

Korin sat there, melted by heat and pleasure. If only this moment could have stretched out forever.

But it couldn't. The whispering voice of reality was creeping in around the edge of Korin's fading bliss. The reminder of where he was and who exactly he was with.

Ádan seemed to feel the change in Korin. He pulled back, giving Korin space, although his hands still rested lightly on Korin's arms. Before Korin could think what to say, Ádan leaned in and whispered, "It isn't morning yet. We're both tired. You could come to bed with me."

It was a terrible idea. The worst idea in all the world. But Korin could only answer, "Yes."

Korin woke with a start, disoriented in the absolute darkness until he remembered where he was. Ádan's room, Ádan's bed, with Ádan.

What time was it? How long had he slept? In the underground room, there was no way to tell.

"Korin," came Ádan's sleepy whisper. His hand slid across Korin's chest, stilling him.

But Korin didn't go back to sleep. He couldn't. Too many thoughts whirling through his head. Regrets and fears and second-guesses. Ádan's fingers moved in light, soothing circles across Korin's skin, a sign that he, too, was awake.

The disembodying darkness made it easy for Korin to ask the question that was pounding against his mind. "How can you be one of them?"

Ádan's hand spread flat over Korin's sternum and Ádan gave a soft sigh. "Do you really want to know?"

"I want to understand."

A rustling sound and the bed sank under Korin as Ádan moved closer. He pulled Korin back against his chest, wrapping his arms around Korin, and Korin wasn't sure if this was for Ádan's reassurance or his own.

"I grew up in Ulek, in the mountains. Not far from the King's castle. My father was a hunter. We sold fur and meat. My mother died in childbirth, and my father's second wife never caught pregnant. I think he blamed me for both these things.

"When I was eleven, he walked in on me in the shed with an older boy from town. He wasn't amused. He threw me out." Ádan's voice sounded detached, like he was reciting a story—one that didn't particularly interest him. "I hadn't been raised with a lot of marketable skills. I couldn't read. I could barely count. I tried stealing; I wasn't good at that either. I got caught and turned over to the authorities at the castle. As it turns out, that was one of the quickest ways to get recruited by the knights."

Ádan's fingers went back to drawing idle patterns on Korin's chest as his voice softened, grew thoughtful. "I know what you think of us. What everyone thinks of us. A lot of it's true. The knights lost their prestige even before we were driven out of Triome. It had been years since we had our pick of recruits. When I joined, most of the knights were like me, outcasts and criminals, driven to the knights because we had no other choice. And if that were the whole of it, I'd be first in line to say we deserved what we got."

Ádan's other hand found Korin's, clung to it. "We were fighting for our life. The world had turned against us. The stories people told—well, you know them. That we summoned demons. Butchered children. Engaged in perverted sexual acts." He paused, and a hint of the more familiar Ádan had crept into his voice when he added, "Well, there may be some truth to that last part."

But he sobered again as he continued his story. "Grandmaster Derian himself saw to my training. He saw that I had talent, that I could be of particular use to the knights. I was trained as a Knight of the Arrow. My order, we were basically spies. In that capacity, I spent a lot of time in Triome, made friends with Prince Lysander. I had letters of introduction from a pile of southern lords and a new family name no one questioned. I fit right in."

Korin shifted, uncomfortable with the talk of deception. Were spies ever simply spies? "Did you kill people?"

Ádan squeezed his hand. "No. Never…I've never…"

He sighed again and sat up, the sudden absence of his body letting cold underground air against Korin's back. "I'm explaining this badly. And it doesn't matter. None of it will make sense without…do you really want to know?"

Korin was in this far. He'd already committed to poor decisions, so what was one more? "Yes."

"Then get dressed. There's something you need to see."

17

*K*ORIN DID AS Ádan asked and followed him out into the safehouse. Back down the stairs that led to the hot springs, but Ádan kept going past that tunnel and into a deeper, longer passage.

All the time, Ádan was talking. "Nikki and V and I, we escaped Ulek. As far as I know, we're the only ones. The knights are dead. I can't afford to be sentimental about that. And honestly, if all we were—if the only thing left of the knights was what we'd fallen to—outlaws and villains tied together with questionable oaths and less and less reason to adhere to them—I'd be the first to say good riddance.

"But we were greater than that once. We were a force for good in the world." Ádan walked with his right hand against the wall, like he was feeling for something. "What do you know about us? About our history?"

Korin had to search his mind for anything that wouldn't be immediately insulting. "That you started out as another order of wizards. Until you decided you didn't need to follow the council's laws."

"I promise you, Korin, we adhere to stricter rules than any wizard."

Korin let that pass. "Most of what I know is old history. What I learned in school. Ulek was yours from the beginning. The King there had been a knight since the start of your order. For a long time, the Knights were strong here in Triome, too. Until they caught you..." Korin realized he wasn't sure what had been the original complaint about the knights. He also realized he didn't care. "I don't know your history, and I don't see how it matters. I was there on the front lines. I saw what the knights did. I know who you are. Were."

"Context, Sunshine. One man's just war is another man's witch hunt. I was there too. I stood next to King Kolyn and Grand-master Derian. I watched them agonize over every decision. The burden of duty—"

"Duty?" Korin interrupted. "Poisoning the land? Slaughtering innocents?"

"Innocents," Ádan scoffed. "What innocents? The wizards? The Darkivels? The vultures who practically perched on Archduke Rhanis's shoulders, waiting to pick apart the remains of Ulek once King Kolyn fell?"

"The innocents," Korin repeated. "The people who had no choice. Who lost their homes and their lives because you couldn't just..."

"Just what? Just surrender? Just turn ourselves over to be executed?"

"Maybe." It was a weak answer, and Korin knew it. This was a terrible argument. Not just because it was upsetting to think about, but because Korin realized, maybe for the first time, he didn't really know the reason for any of it. "You abused your power. Used corrupted magic. Broke laws that have been in effect for centuries—"

"Let me show you," Ádan interrupted, pressing his hand flat

against the wall. "Nothing I say will make sense until you see what the war was really about."

Under Ádan's hand, the solid stone wall rippled. Ádan closed his eyes, as focused and intent as Korin had ever seen him. He pressed forward and the stone dimpled, then parted, melting away like snow under a bright spring sun.

As the wall pulled away, Korin felt it. The power crashed against him, turned his stomach. He flinched back even as he was drawn forward, his feet moving of their own accord. A voice spoke into his mind, the voice from above, only down here, it was much stronger, no longer a whisper. **You've returned.**

Unable to stop himself, Korin walked through the opening in the wall to see what waited on the other side.

THE IMMENSE UNDERGROUND cavern was a wonder in and of itself. Korin stood on a narrow walkway that ran along the wall about thirty feet up from the floor, and the ceiling was at least another thirty feet higher. The walls were covered with magic wards and symbols carved deep into the stone. They gave off a flickering, silvery light by which Korin could see, and yet, as he looked around, he felt like he was surrounded by a darkness so thick he might never find his way out.

At the center of the cavern, rising out of the ground, was a great tree. Its massive trunk was wider than Korin was tall, and its branches spread wide enough to brush the cavern walls with their tips. But the tree was rotting, black and twisted. Dead.

Not dead, the voice spoke to him. **Trapped. We cry. We dream. We hunger**.

The tree pulsed with the rotting energy of the blight. The power that both drew and repulsed Korin. As Korin stared, his eyes telling him that he both could and couldn't see through the darkness, the tree faded, melting into the darkness, and at its center,

Korin saw—the true heart. The source of the roiling decay. "There's a knife sunk into the floor."

"You can see it?" Ádan's voice sounded very far away. The tree was closer. Realer.

Korin. My Korin. Breathe my power. Reach for it. Take it. Claim it.

The magic swirled around Korin, called to him. Brittle black branches reached up towards him. He had only to stretch out his hand to touch them, to soak the power into himself.

Ádan had lied. "You knew what the blight was all along. You knew where it came from."

"No. No, Korin, I swear it. I don't know what's causing the blight."

Was Korin still just reaching for the easy answers? This close, this clear, Korin could see how the tree—the knife was and wasn't the power he'd seen. This was reaching for him, but not in that virulent, destructive way. It was pure death, but also alive in a way Korin could feel to his core but couldn't understand.

Life and death. We are one. You and I, we are the same.

"No," Korin whispered. Not the same.

The knife. The tree. Korin saw both, and neither—blinded by darkness, blinded by the watery light. In this room lived death. Pure, untainted, and raw. It curled around Korin, caressed him, filled the air he breathed. It resonated with the deepest part of his soul.

You see me. You know me, and I know you.

Korin touched one of the branches, felt the brittle wood curve and twist around his fingers. Like a caress.

A memory, pure and sharp, of reaching inside his attackers in Naktigan, of ripping and twisting, how it had felt. That intimate touch, his magic, his power, the life that was his to take. **I was there. I was with you. You called to me and I answered.**

Korin's fists clenched and the branch crumbled in his fingers.

He fled.

. . .

HE DIDN'T MAKE it far. Shaky, his legs could barely carry him. He had to stop. He leaned his forehead against the wall, eyes closed, hands clenched at his sides. He had no idea how long he stood that way, trying to purge all thoughts of the insidious touch of that horrible magic.

From far behind came the grinding sounds of stone reforming. Ádan closing the portal. Then Ádan's footsteps approached, stopped at a cautious distance. Giving Korin space.

"There's always been a secret order within the wizard-knights," Ádan said. "An order with a sacred duty above all else. Grandmaster Derian chose me for the order. I was one of the last. Now I'm the only. That thing in there—the knife, the tree—we were the guardians. For centuries, this has been the heart of our purpose, a purpose kept secret even from most of the Knight orders and certainly from the world.

"It's evil. It's death. It's corruption. And over time, it corrupted us. It destroyed us. Derian—in the end, he sacrificed everything just so I could get away with the knife, bring it back here, where we guarded it from the start. Nikki and V, they didn't know until the night we escaped from Castle Ulek with it.

"The three of us, we're all that's left. And that isn't enough. We need help."

Korin shook his head, reflexive denial, but Ádan kept talking.

"Even if I can rebuild us, even if I can find some way to keep the knife hidden and protected from people who would abuse its power, I can't stop the corruption from happening. The power creeps inside. It's insidious. And it's aware. I know you felt that. Heard it. It wants free, and it will do everything in its power to make that happen.

Ádan touched Korin's shoulder, rested his hand there. "You, Korin. We need you. When I saw you cure the blight in that old man, I knew it. If there's anyone who can figure out a way to protect us, to keep us safe over time—"

"No." Korin turned, pushed Ádan away. "No! I can't. I won't! And you can't ask me to."

"I have to," Ádan answered calmly.

"No." Korin's stomach twisted. He felt sick. "No. Even if I wanted to help you, even if I thought—I'm not the man you want. You don't know me. You don't understand."

Ádan's lips turned up in a sad little smile. "You're not any kind of puzzle, Sunshine. You care for people and it shows. I do know you. I had you figured out the day we first met."

Korin wrapped his arms around himself. How was it so cold down here? "You say you know it talked to me. Do you have any idea what it said? It knows me. It *wants* me. It knows…I can't help you. I can't save you from corruption. I'm already corrupted."

"Bullshit."

"It's true. It's been true all along. In the academy, it's been talking to me. And it felt—" Korin couldn't look Ádan in the face. "I'm a hypocrite. I'm a liar. I hate you and I hate the knights and it's all their fault, but really it isn't. Really, I'm the one who failed. I'm the one who abused my power. I killed. I took lives. And that *thing* in there, it knows." Corruption. Teriad had known. Teriad had warned them.

"You killed people who were trying to kill you."

"There's always an excuse," Korin said, echoing words Teriad has said a hundred times. "Every killer, every abuser, every person who uses the power they have to hurt someone else—they always have an excuse. If I'd been a better man, if I'd been what Teriad—"

"Teriad is dead," Ádan interrupted, his voice flat.

"He died without ever taking a life, without ever using his gift to hurt anyone."

"Oh for fuck's sake!" The explosive frustration in Ádan's voice made Korin look up. "All of you," Ádan continued. "You people. You're all so fucking eager to die for your beliefs. Meanwhile, the assholes just keep going. Which means if you good, *moral* people get your wish, all we have left is a world full of assholes. You ever think of that?

"Teriad's dead. Grandmaster Derian's dead. King Kolyn is dead. And all for what they believed in. Well, good for them. But that doesn't do shit for those of us left behind to clean up their mess. Those of us who are a little less interested in dying dramatically for a cause and a little more focused on keeping the world from ending.

"I'm sick and fucking tired of it. You did what you had to do. Yes, you killed those people. You survived. And that's how you get to be here, with me, and how you get to *keep fighting*. You've got a chance to help people, to keep making things right, and that's something Teriad won't ever be able to do again."

Korin found himself yelling in answer. "I can't help you! I can't be near that…that *thing*. I don't want—" The reminder, the temptation, the memories, the power…

Any of it. "I don't want this." He stared into Ádan's eyes, spoke the final words slow and clear. "I don't want you."

Korin turned and walked away.

Ádan didn't follow.

18

*K*ORIN STUMBLED OUT of the safehouse and into the still-dark city streets. He had no idea what time it was or whether it was safe. He only knew he had to get away from Ádan and the knights and their cursed knife.

"Master wizard?"

The soft, feminine voice was the last thing Korin expected, and at first he couldn't make sense of it. "Hello?"

A young woman, across the street but moving towards him. Out of sheer reflex, he opened his wizard sight and immediately saw the telltale lines of the blight. Barely started in the poor young woman, but unmistakably there.

"Master wizard," she said again. "I'm sorry. I know it's late. But I've been looking for you. I heard you've been helping people. Healing people who are sick like me."

Korin nodded. Off-balanced and confused. "Who are you?"

"Is it true?" She grabbed his hand before he could pull back. "Is it true you can heal people like me?"

"I…yes, but…"

"Oh thank you," she breathed, tugging on his hand. "We need your help. My mother. My brother. They're all sick."

The last twenty-four hours had been so horribly surreal, and this was possibly the strangest moment of all. But Korin's tired, abused mind was slowly kicking back into gear. Taking in what the girl was saying. "Your whole family has it? It's contagious?"

"I don't know. Everyone's so sick. And I heard—people, they said you could help."

"Yes. All right." Too much to think about. But this was something Korin could do and do right. He could think about the rest later. "Take me to your family."

She didn't surrender his hand. Leading him through the quiet, pre-dawn streets. They headed north, towards a part of town he didn't know. The girl's flesh was feverishly warm against Korin's. "I'm so glad I found you. Everyone will be so happy to see you. I'm Aiya," she smiled.

"How long have you been sick?" Korin asked the question automatically. Trying to organize his thoughts—this situation—into a narrative that made sense.

"Sick? Oh, yes, I don't…I'm not sure."

Korin gave her a closer look. Examined her with his wizard sight. Her temperature was high. Her heart rate alarmingly fast. "Do you feel alright? Maybe we should stop."

"No!" She pulled harder against his hand. "No, you have to come with me."

Korin didn't want to upset her. "It's okay. I'm with you." He looked around at the unfamiliar streets she was leading him through. "Where are we going?"

"This way." She squeezed. "It's not much further."

Except it was. They kept walking, past houses and shops, past stables and gardens. Until the buildings grew sparser, the trees thicker, and the street dwindled into a dirt trail.

Aiya was taking Korin outside the city. Out into the jungle. "Where are we going?" Korin asked again.

"It's really not much further," Aiya promised.

This time, she was telling the truth. Korin heard the people before he saw them, a cheerful chattering that blended with the wind through the thick leaves into a pleasant white noise.

Except something about this was off. All those people, talking happily. Awake in the pre-dawn hours. Outside the city, so many...

Aiya called out, "I've brought the wizard!" As she dragged Korin forward into the clearing.

The talking died away. Leaving a strange silence. Something about this was wrong. Very wrong. He followed Aiya into the clearing, saw the people—all the people—and, more important, saw what stood at the center of the clearing.

A tree. Tall, black, twisted, dead. A perfect twin of the tree he'd seen in the cave below the academy.

And the man standing before the tree, with his face shot through with the rotting lines of the blight and the rest of his body blistered and peeling. His eyes were pure black, and his hair was shock white. He raised a hand, pointed, and the blighted power boiled out from him, crossed the clearing, surrounded and swallowed Korin.

It was too much. Korin couldn't make his mind, his body, respond. Smothered by the toxic energy, Korin collapsed and the world went dark.

WHEN KORIN WOKE, he was sitting upright on the ground, tied to the tree, his arms bound tight and flat against the trunk. It was still night. Night again? How long had he been unconscious? The clearing was eerie, full of long, dancing shadows, with only flickering firelight to illuminate it.

Korin quickly closed his eyes again, wanting time to think before anyone noticed he was awake.

Korin ached all over, like he'd been beaten, but the ache came inside out, not outside in. The death magic—the blight, had hurt him at his very core.

He could fix that. Korin let out his breath, focused, called a burst of energy to—

Sudden pain as something solid and heavy struck the side of Korin's head. "None of that," said a raspy voice from outside Korin's range of vision. "I've no interest in breaking you, Korin of the Staff, but I can't have you doing any magic. Care to find out how many blows to the head it takes to make you forget how?"

Korin didn't answer, but he did open his eyes. He tried to look around, but they'd looped rope around his chin and his forehead tight enough he couldn't budge.

"Too scared to talk?" the voice walked into view—the blighted man who had done the magic that knocked Korin out. He crouched down in front of Korin, leaned in close. The energy of the blight seethed and writhed in his skin.

The man grinned, displaying his near-toothless mouth. "No, not scared. I see rebellion on that pretty face." His gaze flicked up, at whoever stood behind Korin. "Plot all you like. Nult there is sensitive to magic. He'll know if you start up any tricks and respond accordingly."

With the previous blow still pounding in his head, Korin wasn't eager to test that statement. "How do you know who I am?"

"We've been watching you. You and your wizard-knight friend. Oh yes, we know about the two of you. Undoing all our good work. I knew you wouldn't be able to resist little Aiya, even after you managed to escape from Nult last night."

Korin threw himself forward against the rope, struggling instinctively before he regained control of himself. Nult—the monster from last night—that monster was behind him.

The blighted man smiled at Korin's flare of panic. "Yes, that's better."

Korin struggled again as the man reached out to touch Korin's cheek in a twisted mockery of a caress. The hand that touched Korin was missing three fingers. "You'll make Her happy. So young. So healthy. How lucky we are you chose to come to

Triome. Staff wizards make the best sacrifices, but I'm afraid we ran out of you."

It was too much to try to wrap his mind around. "I don't understand," Korin whispered, recoiling from the touch as much as his bindings allowed.

"It's all right," the blighted man soothed. "You don't have to."

He stood, moved away, and was replaced in Korin's narrow line of sight by Aiya. "Oh, Korin, thank you," she said, ecstatic. "Thank you for coming here."

How had he missed the fervor in her bright eyes? Or maybe it was only visible now because she wasn't acting anymore. "You lied to me."

She nodded, patted his shoulder. "It's for the best. I promise. It's going to be so beautiful." She sighed. "Since I brought you, your death is mine. I can finally offer a death to the Lady."

"Aiya," snapped the blighted man, off to the side where Korin couldn't see. "Come away from him."

"But he's mine," she whined. "And he's so perfect." She leaned in close, resting her knees on his thighs. "You'll make Her so happy."

The only way Korin could fight his rising panic was to focus on questions, to try to figure this out. "Who are you talking about? What lady?"

"The Lady of the Tree!" Aiya sounded offended that he should have to ask. She reached above his head to stroke the rough bark with a joy on her face that was almost sexual. "The Pale Woman. Mother of snakes. Daughter of the void. She commands death and chaos and everything goes to her in the end. She's the greatest power in the universe." Her voice raised in fevered devotion as she spoke. "The Lady cares nothing for the lies of the Shepherd and the Prophet. The Light has no power over Her. On the day she's made whole again, she'll open her eyes and devour—"

"Aiya!" This time, the blighted man grabbed her by the

shoulder and dragged her back away from Korin, interrupting her increasingly disturbing speech.

"I'm sorry," the blighted man said. "Don't let her upset you. It's better if you can relax."

The absurdity of that statement pierced through the haze of terror that was fogging Korin's brain. "Relax?" To his own ear, his voice sounded clearer, more like himself. "You're planning to kill me."

"Yes, of course. But the Lady prefers her sacrifices…unblemished. No tarnish to their potential. Plus it's more comfortable for you, don't you think?"

The veneer of reason had hidden it, but the blighted man was every bit as far gone as Aiya.

Korin's fear broke, leaving a cool sense of clarity in his mind. For the first time since he and Ádan had been attacked in the street, he felt sharp, alert, *there*. He couldn't afford any more time wasted on panic. On confusion. On regrets and second-guesses. He had to think.

He was immobilized. The ropes were tight and wrapped thick all up and down his body. He'd lost feeling in his arms, which was probably for the best given the angle they were pulled back around the tree. They were going to hurt. Assuming he ever had the chance to feel them again.

Magic—a quick strike he could probably pull off before the monster behind him could react. But…what? Even if he freed himself or—and Korin's mind flinched at the thought—killed Aiya or the blighted man, Nult was still back there. And Nult hadn't been affected by any magic Korin had thrown at him.

What did that leave?

Nothing. Korin could do nothing.

He could give up. With that thought came the memory of Ádan, full of rage at the idea that surrender was preferable to pushing back. Anger at those who had laid down their lives instead of fighting on.

Korin didn't know how to resist, but he knew he wanted to. He wasn't ready to give up. He believed, as had Teriad, that life was something greater, something worth fighting for. He wasn't ready to stop.

Because that was what Teriad had done. He'd given up. Offered up not just his own life, but Jon's and Lia's as well. Had they been given a choice? Or had they just followed Teriad blindly? As Korin would have if he hadn't already been sent away?

Korin felt guilty, responsible, but more than that he was angry. At the knights, yes. At himself, absolutely. But mostly at Teriad. Because if Teriad had truly believed in life, in fighting always for life, that would have included fighting for Jon and for Lia. For Teriad himself.

For Korin.

Korin had made a mistake. A desperate mistake. And Teriad had sent him away. There'd been no second chance, no benefit of the doubt, no forgiveness for the apprentice who had followed him with absolute loyalty and obedience for five whole years.

Teriad had given up on him.

Korin wanted to live. Wanted desperately to live. And how was that different from anyone?

The sudden fury brought on by this train of thought made Korin tense up, push against the rope.

The blighted man saw. His eyes narrowed. "Nult, show him—"

That was all he got out before a flash of blinding light exploded in the clearing.

19

*K*ORIN EXPECTED THE blow, but it didn't come. He didn't question, didn't think, but pulled a wave of bright energy through himself to erase all the damage the blighted man's magic had done to him.

The ropes fell away. Not from anything he'd done. It startled Korin, but he reacted on instinct, scrambling from the tree. As he pushed away, he looked back and saw Nult, a heavy stick raised in mid-swing, struggling against it as though some invisible person stood beneath him, holding it up.

Or as though someone were using magic.

Korin scanned around, taking in the scene as fast as he could. There were more people than he'd realized. In the light of the fires that ringed the clearing, he counted Aiya, the blighted man, and five more. Plus Nult beside the tree, and the other horrifying monstrosity lumbering over to help him.

"Get him! Get the wizard!" the blighted man shouted and the creature turned its attention to Korin.

A knife whistled through the air and sunk deep into the center of the blighted man's chest. A knife Korin recognized. Ádan's. The blighted man looked down, a frown that was more annoyance than pain on his face. "Come out, come out," he called in a singsong voice as the rest of the blighted man's people spread around the fires, brandishing sticks and knives, searching for their attackers.

Korin tried to get to his feet, ready to run, but with his attention split between the blighted man and the monster approaching him, he was caught off guard by an attack from a different direction. Aiya tackled him from behind. "You're mine!" she screamed. "Mine!"

They rolled together, struggling. She was stronger than she looked. Stronger than she should have been. She pinned Korin face-down on the ground, her hands on his wrists, knees on his back. "She'll have you," Aiya hissed. "She'll know my loyalty."

Searing cold at every place she touched him. It froze. It burned. It was agony. The deadly magic of the blight in its purest form. Aiya was forcing it into Korin, driving the magic through him. Korin could feel it dissolving his flesh, rotting him from the outside in. Killing him.

It would have killed him, if Korin had never touched this magic before. Aiya's power was brutal and fast. It gave him no time to think. If Korin hadn't already developed an instinctive response to the crippling invasive corruption, he would have been lost.

But Korin had fought the blight. Korin had healed the blight. As his body screamed at the pain, Korin's magic instinctively launched a counter-attack.

It wasn't enough. The blight had been insidious, but undirected. With Aiya's hands on him, her power focused on him and only him, Korin was overwhelmed. Every inch she gained was more pain, another part of him lost to agony. Lost to the invasive, twisted power.

And then it was gone. Aiya was gone. Without resistance, Korin's magic ripped back through his own body, undoing the damage Aiya had done. All as he rolled over, struggling to sit up and see what happened.

Ádan was there. Ádan had broken cover to pull Aiya off Korin.

He'd saved Korin, but as Korin watched, Ádan collapsed beneath Aiya's hands which radiated putrid, decaying power.

Before Korin could make a move to help, Nult's club slammed into his shoulder and he was knocked back down to the ground. Nult lifted the weapon again, ready to bring it down on Korin's head, but it froze in the air like it was stuck. Korin turned his head to the side and saw Nikki next to one of the fires, one hand extended like he was pushing up against the club, the sweat of his exertion rolling down his face. But two more of the blighted people were closing in on him from behind. In the opposite direction, Varajas danced with the other brute, a flaming sword in his hand, a look of fierce concentration on his face as the fire behind writhed and flared in a flaming cage that held two more of the blighted people.

"Korin!" Ádan yelled, his voice rough and breaking. Aiya's magic was tearing him apart, the same as it had Korin. Only Ádan had none of Korin's defenses.

None of the knights did. Whatever magic they had, whatever skill as warriors, they were helpless against this withering magic these men and women had summoned. Outmatched by the same malevolent power they were supposed to be guarding against.

Korin scrambled forward, out from under Nult. He reached out for Aiya, was just able to grab her calf. He couldn't reach Ádan, but he flooded Aiya with magic, pushing pure healing power through her with enough force it should keep going into Ádan. Now it was Aiya's turn to scream.

Aiya dropped Ádan and kicked free of Korin's hand. She turned her power back on Korin, but he had the advantage this time. She couldn't push past his wall of power. He treated her like he had Dustin and Shaiera, like a victim of the blight, sending sparks of healing energy through her body to drive away the darkness.

Everything else fell away. The clearing, the battle. Nult, the blighted man. Ádan and the other knights. All Korin knew was

Aiya and the twisting energy inside her, every searching tendril and writhing thread. Korin grabbed her hands, held them tight.

Korin healed her.

She screamed again and fell to her knees. She reached out for Korin as she had before, but the blight was gone from inside her and it seemed her power was gone as well.

That was the answer. That was why they'd come after Korin, why they'd targeted wizards of his order. The blight wasn't the result of their power. It was the source of it.

Ádan was still on the ground, unmoving. But before Korin could get to him, monstrous hands grabbed Korin's arms and yanked him into the air with implacable strength. Korin's shoulders popped out of their sockets with a throbbing pain as he kicked and struggled. He was trapped. No way he could escape Nult's hold through any physical means.

But now Korin knew how to fight back. The pain was distracting, but no worse than what Korin had already faced today. He focused around it, to the hands like iron on his arms.

The blight had a stronger hold on Nult. It had reshaped Nult into the monster he was, stretched him, grown him, and filled him. But in doing so, it had weakened him. Parts of him were all blight. No wonder had hadn't noticed or cared about any of the damage Ádan and Korin had tried to do to him. His blood, his guts, his very heart were sludgy messes of rot radiating out the magic of death.

If Korin could—

"Hold the wizard!" The blighted man yelled at Nult. Korin's head whipped around to see what was happening. The blighted man had pulled Ádan's knife out of himself, but his attention was on Nikki, not Korin. Nikki, his own flaming sword in hand, who had beheaded one of his attackers and now danced in and out of the reach of the other blighted brute, harassing him with quick, searing slices.

The blighted man grabbed Aiya by the hair. She was still

sobbing, but she didn't pull away. In fact, she turned her face up to him, mouthed, "Yes."

He brought the knife straight down.

A fountain of blood soaked his arm and splattered on his face. The blighted man laughed wildly. With Aiya's encroaching death, the power within him grew.

In a matter of seconds, that power would be directed at Nikki, at Varajas, at Ádan, who had no defenses against it.

But only if Aiya died.

Korin couldn't touch her, could barely see through the haze of his own pain. But he'd healed her once already. His magic knew the shape of her.

Korin closed his eyes, tried to shut out everything else. With all the force of his will, he summoned into being the Aiya that had been there only moments ago. An Aiya who wasn't fountaining blood, who wasn't choking on her own bodily fluids, who wasn't dying.

She screamed. The blighted man stabbed her again. Korin felt the piercing force of the knife like it was cutting through his own body. He pushed back, knitting lungs and blood vessels and flesh back together.

"Kill the wizard!" The blighted man screamed, full of fury. "Kill—"

His shriek cut off. Korin looked to see Ádan—alive and standing—with a wire pulled tight around the blighted man's neck. It wouldn't work, Korin wanted to call out, but he couldn't get the air. Nult, obedient, was squeezing Korin between his two giant hands. Crushing him.

A flaming dagger tumbled through the air from across the clearing, buried itself in the blighted man's stomach. From the corner of his eye, Korin could just see Nikki's look of fierce concentration as the flames spread and engulfed the man. Ádan pulled away as the man's skin blackened and melted in the magical fire. The blighted man collapsed to the ground. Even the magic of death couldn't save him from that.

Nult froze, then dropped Korin. Korin gasped for breath as the enraged monster rushed Ádan.

More magic spun around Nult. Not from Korin. Korin could hardly make sense of what was happening. Ádan dodged Nult's wide swing as Nult tripped, like someone had just shoved his shoulder. Varajas darted in from one side as Nikhil came up from the other. The three knights moved in and out, a chaotic dance that Korin's exhausted mind couldn't follow. He knew how to fight Nult, but he couldn't find the words to say it.

Dimly, he was aware of the rest of the group fleeing into the dark jungle. Of Aiya spitting at him, then running. Of Ádan and his friends whittling away at Nult with a skill and grace that would have been beautiful if Korin could just keep his eyes open. But as adrenaline faded and pain and exhaustion took its place, Korin was losing the battle for consciousness.

He lay down. Easier that way. He heard his name, but he didn't have the energy to respond.

Korin fell into darkness.

20

KORIN WOKE UP in his bed at Marta's. He was wearing different clothes than he had been. The sun was shining in through the window. He was thirsty, hungry, and he hurt all over.

The door was opening. That was what had woken him up, the scrape of the lock turning.

"Oh!" Lily was in the doorway, a tray in her hand. "You're awake!"

Korin tried to sit up, but a wave of dizziness and nausea hit him. "Oh no, let me help." Lily rushed over to the bed, setting the tray down on the dresser. Korin could see a bowl and a washcloth.

With Lily's help, Korin managed his way upright, leaning against the wall. "What happened? How did I get here? What day is it?"

Lily pulled the chair over and sat down next to Korin's bed. "Lord Ádan brought you in two nights ago. He got you all cleaned up and put to bed. He and Marta had a talk. You haven't been awake, but Marta's had us give you broth, as we could."

The concern in her voice was clear. "Lord Ádan, he said you'd be better. But me an' Verania and Holli, we were real worried. It's good to see you with your eyes open."

Korin smiled at her. "It's good to see you, too. Thank you for looking after me."

"Marta, she's been upset. And Lord Ádan keeps coming around to see if you've woke up yet." A smile grew on her lips. "He's handsome. And nice. I like him."

Korin chose not to comment on that. "Is that more soup you brought me?"

"Yeah. Though if you want, I can bring you anything. And Marta'll want to see you. If you're up to it."

Korin closed his eyes and reached for his magic. Exhausted and dizzy, the power was slippery. Potentially dangerous. He wouldn't dare try to use it on anyone else, but this was his own body. He didn't so much have to focus and control as just relax and let the power flow into its well-worn pattern.

Magic filled him, warm and soft and familiar. The aches faded to a dull throb. The dizziness went away. He was still tired, and more than a little sore. Fixing those things would require real concentration that he didn't have right now. But he felt ready to face the world again. "I'd love some rice and whatever meat you've got cooking. And some juice to drink. And if Marta needs to talk to me, I'm here."

Lily nodded and stood. After a moment's dithering, she leaned over and pressed a quick kiss to Korin's forehead.

She left the bowl of broth, which Korin gratefully sipped from his seat in bed. He stared at the blank wall across from him, letting his mind float in an almost meditative state. He wasn't ready to think about anything, to ask the questions he was going to have to ask. He was grateful for the chance to sit here in his quiet room where it was warm and safe and nothing was more complicated than he wanted it to be.

Marta opened the door without knocking. She stood in the doorway, arms cross, looking him up and down. "You're better."

"I'm getting there." Korin set his bowl down on the night-stand. "I'm sorry to be so much inconvenience."

"You looked something like death when that noble boy brought you in. What trouble did he drag you into?"

A sharp, harsh laugh forced its way out before Korin could stop it. He covered his mouth. Trouble. Where even to begin? "It isn't like you think. There was a disease. I was healing people. Some others took exception."

Marta's eyes narrowed. She knew she wasn't getting the whole story. But Korin didn't elaborate.

"I'm sorry if I've been in the way," Korin said. "I'll be up and around soon. I don't need the girls—"

"Shush." Marta pointed a scolding finger at him. "None of that. We look after our own in this house."

Korin didn't know what to say to that. "I don't want to take advantage."

Marta rolled her eyes. "Boy, you don't have it in you to take advantage. So stop talking nonsense. I told you, you've got a home here as long as you want it. So lie down, get some sleep, and get better."

Pulling the door shut behind her with some force, Marta left Korin there. He heard her stomp down the stairs and yell for Verania. It was a pleasant, familiar sound.

It had been so long. School had always felt temporary. Teriad had never stayed long in one place. The idea that he could stay here, be welcome here, among friends who worried about him and would miss him if he were gone—it was almost too much.

But when Lily came back up the stairs with a delicious lunch, and stayed and talked to him while he ate. When Verania popped her head in just to check up on him as she was working. When Holli brought him a sweet almond roll and said Marta had sent her out for it, Korin smiled and thanked them. Like friends. Like family.

Like home.

. . .

After a solid meal and another nap, Korin was almost back to himself. He took a long soak in the bathtub, daring enough magic to keep the water hot. It made him think of the springs beneath the knights' academy. It made him think of Ádan.

Lily brought him some dinner, which he ate in his room, flipping idly through one of the library books without really paying attention to the words on the page. His window shutters were open, and Korin was content in the warm breeze blowing through, listening to the soft evening sounds of the city.

He was surprised, then, when Ádan swung in through his window. As he had that night that now seemed ages ago.

"There's a door, you know," Korin said, as he had before.

Ádan grinned and repeated his own words. "What fun would that be?"

Ádan looked as good as ever. Whatever had happened out there in the jungle after Korin had passed out, Ádan had come out well. Still, Korin asked, "Are you alright? Did everyone...? Nikki and Varajas?"

"Never better. And eager to see you again once you're ready. Even Nikki. Not that he'd say so. I swear, he's never so happy as when he's pissed at someone."

So strange to be sitting here, after everything. Korin wasn't sure what to say, what he wanted to say. Where even to start? "Thank you. For saving my life."

Ádan crossed the small room and sat down on the end of Korin's bed. He made himself comfortable, leaning back against the wall, but Korin noticed Ádan had arranged himself in a way that put distance between them. "I came here—two days ago, I mean—to apologize. I shouldn't have blindsided you with the knife like that. Except you weren't here. No one had seen you. It took Nikki and V and I the whole day to find anyone who'd been awake to see you with that girl and who knew which way you went. I was terrified we'd find you dead."

"I'm still a little surprised you didn't." Like infection in a wound, most of Korin's anger had drained away. He understood, now, how much of his anger at Ádan had really been anger at Teriad. Anger at himself. "I'm sorry too. For leaving like that. It wasn't all about you."

Ádan's perpetual smile faltered. He looked tired. "Listen, I wanted to tell you, you don't owe me anything. You were right when you said I shouldn't have asked you to help us. If you want to walk away, I understand. I won't stop you."

Korin had nothing left in him but honesty. "I don't know what I want."

Except was that true? In the madness of the past couple weeks —discovering and dealing with the blight, getting to know the city, his fights with Nikki, with Ádan, the secrets he'd learned— there'd been anchor points of happiness. "I want to help people. I want to heal people. It's what I'm good at."

Ádan nodded. "That's a good thing to want." He stood up, patting Korin's foot as he did so. "Get some rest, Sunshine."

A good-bye if Korin had ever heard one.

But Korin wasn't done. "I want you," he said in a voice barely above a whisper.

Ádan stopped, closed his eyes. "Korin, I'm not sure—"

"Neither am I. About much of anything. I don't know about the blight, or those people who were causing it. I don't know about the knights or that thing you're guarding. I don't know that I want any part of it. But you, Ádan, I don't want to walk away from you."

"I don't want you to," Ádan confessed softly, eyes still closed.

"So what do we do?"

Ádan turned back to face Korin, his smile and self-possession firmly back in place. "Right now, you rest and get better. That's what you do. As for everything else…" He shrugged. "We'll figure it out."

In two steps, he'd closed the distance between them. He slid a hand through Korin's hair as he leaned down and brushed his lips against Korin's in a whisper of a kiss. "I'll see you tomorrow," he promised.

Ádan left and Korin lay back down.

Korin was alive and warm and comfortable. For the first time in weeks—maybe in years—he wasn't afraid. Maybe he should be. Certainly, he had a better understanding now of the evil that moved through the world—through his new home—than he had just a few days ago.

Teriad had been afraid. Korin could see that now. Teriad had wrapped himself so tight in his rules of right and wrong that in the end, they'd strangled him. And Korin had failed Teriad, but in the end, Teriad had failed Korin.

Korin had buried himself in Teriad's rules, in Teriad's disappointment. But as Ádan so eloquently stated, Teriad was dead. And Korin wasn't. Maybe it was time for Korin to figure out what *he* believed. To find the right and wrong that made sense to him, and stop living in the constant fear of disappointing a dead man.

Before Korin could figure out all the rest—Ádan and the knights and the blight and the tree—Korin was going to have to figure out himself. But not today. Today he would rest and recover and simply be happy to be alive.

For today, that was enough.

ABOUT THE AUTHOR

Growing up in a house that included a library of thousands of science fiction and fantasy books, Barbara J. Webb had no choice but to become a writer herself.

A midwesterner at heart, Barbara has lived in Missouri, Kansas, and Arkansas, but finally settled in only two blocks away from the house in which she was born. She enjoys her small-town life with her husband and her cat, and occasionally dreams of keeping horses. Or even better, unicorns.

In addition to writing, Barbara enjoys cooking (her chocolate chip cookies are always in high demand), crochet, and video games. She's been an avid role-playing-gamer since she was ten. Like most of her family, Barbara began music training when she was very young, and has played violin with the Columbia Civic Orchestra, the Missouri Symphony, and several local bands.

Find more of Barbara's books and news at
barbarajwebb.com

Sign up for her newsletter at
buttondown.email/bjwebb

ACKNOWLEDGMENTS

So much love and thanks to Kij Johnson and Lane Robins, who have been with me on this writing journey from the start.

And to Luke Tolvaj, one of my absolute favorite people, who in addition to all his other delightful qualities, is incredibly patient regarding my non-traditional relationship with grammar.

To my fellow residents of the Manor of Pain: Rachael, Rebecca, Izzy, and Corey. We've been to Hell and back together. You keep me energized and inspired in this less-than-perfect world.

My lovely CSSF and Novel Architect workshoppers, past and present. Every summer, you all teach me as much as I teach you.

As ever, to my husband Seth, who is always there for me.

FURTHER READING

Korin and Ádan's story continues in
TWISTED LOYALTIES
Book 2 of Knights of the Twisted Tree

Releasing December 2024

Read on for an excerpt.

CHAPTER 1

*K*orin had learned to live with nightmares. It had taken only a few days on the warfront for them to start, and they'd been a part of his life ever since.

The voices were always the same. The screams, the sobs, the moans. People in pain, suffering. Korin could hear them, could see them, could stand among them, but he could never help. Every time he tried, every time he reached out to touch, they would crumble and blow away like ashes on the wind.

So he walked across the blood-soaked battlefield. On the earth scorched black by fire and magic. Through people who were twitching piles of scorched flesh, others who had been literally torn apart, people with sword wounds and axe wounds, with crushed bones and caved skulls, drowning in pools of their own blood. All crying out to him. Begging. Pleading. For help. For release.

Korin could do nothing.

At the center of it all stood a tree. Bare. Twisted. Dead. Under a moonless sky, it cast its shadow over the dead, reaching fingers of gnarled darkness that touched each and every body. As Korin walked towards the tree, those same shadows criss-crossed his own body, scratched at his skin, caught in his hair.

A tendril of shadow reared up at Korin's approach, resolving into an enormous snake, pale as a ghost. It oozed the decaying energy of the blight. Korin met its silver serpent eyes. The snake, she—for it was a she—slid down the tree and onto Korin's outstretched arm.

They suffer. The snake spoke in Korin's mind. The voice of the knife, the voice of the tree. The voice of death.

Korin stood still as the snake wrapped around him, settling her weight across his shoulders and around his waist. All the while, his attention was on the battlefield, on the tortured, the dying. "I can't help them."

The snake responded to the sadness in Korin's voice, rubbed her head against his face. Her scales were warm and surprisingly soft. **We can help them. You and I. Together.**

Korin knew it was wrong. The snake—the tree—they couldn't help. They could only destroy. The blight, it was worse than anything the people on the battlefield suffered. And yet... and yet...

There's nothing to fear. You love these people, and so do I.

"No," Korin whispered. "You don't love them. You torture them. You kill them."

The serpent stroked his face again, a gentle touch, despite the prickling cold of the blight. **They don't understand. They fear my power, but that makes it no less a gift.** The serpent's tail wound around Korin's arm, lifting it with irresistible strength. **Show them, Korin. Show them my love. Show them yours.**

Power flowed from Korin's hand, life and death twined together. His power, the tree's power, merged as one. It spread across the field, a cloud of energy that left silence everywhere it touched.

Korin tried to stop it, tried to close his hand, but he couldn't. He opened his mouth to scream, but the snake darted in, filling his mouth, his throat. Its power moved over him, through him, the blight eating away at him from the inside.

Dragging him down into darkness.

"HOLD STILL. This won't hurt. I promise." Korin gave his best reassuring smile to the terrified little girl. He looked up at the girl's mother who wore a similarly stricken look as she held her daughter tight as she could while allowing Korin access to the girl's broken arm.

This was a greenstick break, fresh and clean. The bone hadn't pushed through the skin, and the mother had known to bring the girl straight away to Korin. An easy fix.

Korin took the little girl's wrist in one hand and laid his other hand across the break as lightly as he could. He closed his eyes and focused, reaching into the arm with his magic. The first thing he did was pinch around the nerves at the little girl's shoulder to dull the pain.

The little girl gasped, and the shocked terror relaxed into sobbing tears. Korin worked fast while mother and daughter both were focused on her crying. The old shape of the arm was there. The bone remembered how it was supposed to be. Korin focused on that shape and fed a burst of energy into the girl's arm.

With an audible snap, the bone popped back into place, as solid and true as if it had never been broken. The little girl screeched with surprise and tried to jerk away, but Korin held tight to her wrist. He still needed to repair the rest of the damage, realign flesh and muscle and torn blood vessels back to where they should be. "Just a little bit more," he murmured, as soothing as he could manage from the half-trance of magic. "And then you'll be back to climbing trees."

Attuned to her body, Korin felt the chemical jolt of new fear at the mention of trees. Maybe she wouldn't be so quick to go climbing again. Which would be sad, if this trauma scarred her emotionally when Korin had made sure it wouldn't do so physically. But children were resilient and…wait.

There was something not quite right. What was it? An…echo, maybe. A twinge of something as Korin was searching for the arm as it had been, moving through the feel of the injury itself.

And now he was alert, he noticed other things. Like the fact the girl had no bruising anywhere else on her body. If she'd fallen out of a tree, as she'd claimed, there should be some amount of injury elsewhere, even if it was only superficial.

Korin's first worried thought was that someone had broken the girl's arm—an abuse she was afraid to say. Except that would leave bruising too. Maybe not visible, but Korin would be able to see the broken capillaries and crushed skin from hands gripping too tight or a sudden blow.

No, it was as if this girl's arm had just snapped all on its own. With no outside force marking her skin in any other way. Which wasn't possible.

Unless that strange little echo Korin felt was magic. Someone else's magic. Another wizard had done this.

"All better," Korin said, opening his eyes. As he let go, he released the nerves so the girl could feel again. If he'd done his job right—and he had—there would be nothing left to cause her pain.

The little girl was still crying, but now had both her arms wrapped around her mother, giving no sign that either one was causing her any trouble. "Thank you," the mother said, sincere, but awkward. She couldn't meet Korin's eyes, and was already gathering herself to stand.

Because once he was done healing them, they always remembered he was a wizard.

Korin was used to it. He stood, giving her the polite excuse to do the same. The woman was definitely nervous of him, and the little girl was still terrified. And maybe there was nothing unusual about that, or maybe… "Can I ask…did you see her fall?"

The mother shook her head, and her eyes slid away from Korin's, guilty and afraid. Korin didn't know what to make of it and when he said nothing else, the woman lifted her daughter and left without another word, winding her way around the chairs and tables that filled the bar side of the guesthouse.

Since the bar wasn't open yet, Marta—the guesthouse's owner —let Korin use the room to deal with anyone who came to him for help. It was quieter than the always-busy kitchen and meant Korin didn't have to take strangers up to his room.

Korin had been here not-quite a month and word of his presence was spreading through the neighborhood—through the whole city. People were getting to know his skill as a healer and— more importantly—the fact he gave his magic away for free, unlike the Wing wizards who lived in the nicer parts of town and charged more money per healing than Korin had ever seen in his life.

Korin stretched. This morning had been a busy one. In addition to the little girl, he'd seen three men with injuries that had gotten infected, an old woman with a broken hip, and a boy with a stomach virus Korin was going to have to keep an eye out for in case it spread. A solid morning's work.

Korin had never stayed in one place for this long. It was a little scary to think that he was gaining a reputation, that people were learning his name.

He turned to see Verania standing in the door that led back to the kitchen. She wore a bright smile on her pretty face and held a steaming bowl of chicken and rice in her hands. "Thought you might be hungry after all that."

Korin returned her smile. The upside of lingering in one place —friends. People who cared who he was and how he was. People he could like. People he could trust. "Thanks, Verania."

She brought him the food, made him sit back down, went back to the kitchen to find him something to drink. All the girls who worked here liked to fuss over him. Marta, too, in her own surly way. It made Korin feel like he belonged. It made him feel like he was home.

Verania returned with a tall glass of pineapple juice, which was Korin's current favorite. "Anything else you need?" she asked.

Korin smiled and shook his head. Verania gave a wink and a twirl, making her bright skirts swirl wide as she left. Flirting. Not seriously. Marta had made it clear from the first day Korin had moved in that she didn't approve of fraternizing.

Not that Korin would have been interested. Not in the girls. And besides, he had someone.

Maybe. Sort of.

Korin couldn't hold back his smile when he thought of Ádan. Handsome Ádan with his bright grins and irrepressible cheer. Dangerous Ádan with his secrets and his oaths to people Korin didn't know how to trust. Ádan who had saved Korin's life, but in doing so, had pulled Korin into the middle of a horrible secret Korin didn't know if he could face.

Ádan who had now been away for two weeks, summoned by Prince Lysander zhi Ritalle to join the prince in his entourage. Lysander had been in Ulek, at the war front, but he wanted his friend next to him on the journey home. As Ádan had apologetically reported to Korin before riding off.

Korin missed him. Korin didn't miss him. Korin wanted him back right now. Korin thought it might be better if he never saw Ádan again.

But mostly, Korin filled his days with helping the people who came to him. There'd been no sense obsessing when Ádan was away and Korin couldn't do anything about it.

Now Korin had a new question to worry about—what *had* happened to that little girl? Was he imagining things, or…was it possible a wizard had done that? If so, why? And who?

Korin finished his food, took the dishes back to the kitchen, then stuck his head into Marta's office. She sat at her desk, working her way through a ledger, a woman of unguessable age with greying black hair and a will of iron. "What is it, Korin?" she asked without looking up.

"You need anything from me today?"

She stopped with a finger on the last line she'd been studying, looked up at him, considering. "No, I think we're good. You going out?"

"I was going to go to the parade."

She grunted, dismissive of the whole idea. "Go on with you. You got money?"

"Enough. I'll be fine."

She grunted again and returned her attention to the book. Finished with him.

Korin was out the door before anyone else could show up to stop him.

CHAPTER 2

*C*rowds had already gathered along the parade route. It seemed like everyone in Triome had turned up. Korin had never seen so many people all in one place. On the streets, packed into balconies, at windows, along rooftops.

Smells of spicy chicken and roasting cinnamon made Korin's stomach rumble, despite that he'd just eaten. The food in Triome had been a revelation, and Korin had yet to stop being amazed by it.

Korin squeezed through the back of the crowd, moving up the street, but couldn't find any gaps offering a good vantage point. It hadn't occurred to him there would be this many people. It hadn't occurred that there *could* be this many people.

Something stung his neck, and Korin slapped reflexively. The insects here were another new thing, although most of the time they ignored him. Except there wasn't anything there. Korin was lowering his hand just as something small and hard struck his knuckle. This time, he saw the pebble bounce away as it fell. Then a third struck his shoulder.

Korin looked around. Was someone throwing rocks at him?

But no one seemed to be paying him any attention. His eyes scanned the crowd. He looked all around. Then up.

Two buildings down, on the second story roof of a manor walled off from the street, was a face Korin recognized. A handsome, firstborn face on a solid, warrior's body. One of the knights, although not the one Korin most wanted to see.

Varajas waved, beckoning Korin to join him on the roof.

Getting there proved an interesting challenge. There were no obvious places to climb the wall that existed to keep people out of the gardens surrounding this house. Korin had to run and jump, catching the top of the wall with his fingertips, and scrabble up before he lost his grip. He crept nervously through the lush green garden, certain he wasn't supposed to be there. A sturdy trellis got him to the top of the first story, and from there he had to ease along a narrow eave to reach the part of the second story roof that sloped down low enough to grab, then pull himself up again.

A few weeks ago, Korin wouldn't have been able to do this. He'd been ragged, exhausted, first from hard travel and war, and then from a brutal encounter with destructive magic. But time healed all wounds, especially when one was a wizard like Korin. A few quiet weeks of rest and recovery, coupled with the steamy Spring weather and as much delicious food as he could eat and Korin was in possibly the best shape of his life.

Varajas waited for Korin, nodded as Korin carefully crossed the central peak, then worked his way down the slope to join him. Varajas wore a light cloth wrap around his head, protection from the sun, but also a convenient way to hide his face. He'd pulled the cloth back up over his nose, so only his eyes were visible.

"Were you throwing rocks at me?" Korin asked as he sat down.

"Got your attention."

In truth, Korin was surprised Varajas had wanted him up here at all. It wasn't like they were friends. Korin knew the knights' secrets—the most important of which being the fact that they still existed at all. The rest of the world thought they were dead, defeated two months ago in Ulek, at the end of a war that still gave Korin nightmares. But Varajas, along with Ádan and Nikki had escaped the final blows and made it to Triome, dragging a horrible, dangerous burden along with them.

"You're looking better," Varajas commented.

The last time Varajas had seen Korin had been at the end of a fight against monsters who had almost taken Korin's life. Varajas, Ádan, and Nikki had saved Korin. "I never got a chance to thank you—"

Varajas waved away Korin's thanks. "It's a nice day. No reason to talk about that."

Korin couldn't argue. The bright afternoon sun was tempered by the cool, salty breeze coming in off the ocean. Up here, neither the noise nor the smell of the crowds below was overwhelming. Korin had a fleeting regret that he hadn't stopped to grab some of the cinnamon almonds a vendor below was selling, fresh roasted and fragrant, but it wasn't worth climbing back down to get them.

Cheers rippled through the crowd as the leading edge of the parade came into view. Acrobats in bright flowing silks leaped and tumbled, graceful and colorful as exotic birds. "Oh," Korin breathed.

Varajas snorted. "Don't get out much, do you?"

"I've never seen anything like this." Most of Korin's life had been spent in small, remote towns and villages in the freezing south. Or the small, remote school where he'd learned to be a wizard. Or at war.

"This is just the warm-up," Varajas said. "Getting the crowd excited so they'll cheer properly for the people who matter."

Korin didn't know what to say to that, so he just kept watching. After the acrobats came music, flutes and drums and pipes, and behind the musicians, dancers draped in flashing crystal jewelry and little else.

More acrobats and a man breathing fire. An army of dancers in bright feathers. A flame wizard surrounded by twirling women whose bodies sparked with illusionary fire as they moved.

It was all magic to Korin.

The cheers of the crowd swelled to a roar as the first riders came around a bend in the street. "Behold the conquering heroes," Varajas muttered, bitter.

At the front of the line, bejeweled and glamorous, as if they had appeared out of some legend, riding side by side on prancing horses of matching black, Archduke Rhanis zhi Darkivel and his daughter, Archwizard Sheluna of the Wing. Their golden hair flowed bright in the tropical sun as they waved at their cheering audience. The Archduke was old, over one hundred and fifty years, but firstborn aged slowly and gracefully, and he more resembled some fabled warrior prince than a man nearing the end of his prime. Sheluna was a wizard—was the Archwizard—of the only order that knew as much about shaping the body as did Korin's own. Which meant she was exactly as beautiful as she wanted to be, and what she clearly wanted to be was breathtaking. Both were dressed in striking blacks, shining gold, and the dark, rich sapphire color that was known from south to north as Darkivel blue.

The Darkivels. The heroes who had tirelessly led fifty years of brutal warfare to save the world from the demonic scourge of the knights, their Grandmaster, and their King.

"I hate them," Varajas whispered.

Korin didn't know what to think. The world, as he was learning, was more complicated than he had ever realized in his time spent on the warfront dealing with the results of the vicious tactics both sides had leveraged.

Behind the Darkivels rode a man with iron-gray hair, dressed in silver-threaded black. Korin didn't recognize the man's face, but he knew the meaning of the twin swords at the man's hips and the Prophet's cross hanging from his neck. "Is that High Father Donatien?"

"Of course it is," Varajas answered. "Who else would be riding with the snakes?"

Korin flinched at the word *snake*, and shivered under the hot afternoon sun. He glanced at Varajas, but V's attention was still on the parade. He didn't seem to have meant anything significant. Nor had he noticed Korin's reaction. Korin looked back down at Donatien, leader of the Bladed Brothers, the militant arm of the church.

Korin had seen plenty of Blades on the warfront. He'd kept his distance, as had any wizard with sense. The Brothers had been there to fight against the knights, but they specialized in killing the gifted, whether those gifted were wizard-knights or order-sworn wizards. Donatien and all his followers were on good terms with Archwizard Sheluna, which should have meant they were harmless to any wizard who kept their oath, but there were whispers. There were always whispers.

An ordered column of Blades rode behind their High Father, pulling a "Shit," out of Varajas.

"What?"

Varajas shook his head. "Nothing. Just…Blades in the city. Could be trouble."

Something in Varajas's voice sounded off, but before Korin could ask another question, he was distracted.

Behind the Blades, a completely different group. Dressed in bright colors, their horses prancing and sidestepping with restless energy, the vivid opposite of the tight, disciplined column they followed. Korin's stomach gave a flip as he recognized one of them. "Is that Ádan?"

Varajas rolled his eyes. "Of course it is," he said with the same flat disapproval as he'd expressed for High Father Donatien and the Darkivels.

"He's back." Korin couldn't keep the excitement out of his voice.

"Along with the prince." Varajas pointed at the man to Ádan's right. A firstborn in bright gold mail on a bright gold horse, a flashing smile on his sharply handsome face as he waved to the crowd. "Lysander, the Darkivels, High Father Donatien, and Ádan. This city isn't big enough."

Korin was only half-listening. He couldn't take his eyes off Ádan. He looked like a prince himself. Dressed in silver and black leathers that molded perfectly to his muscular frame, Ádan stood tall in his stirrups, urging his horse to a prancing trot. He laughed in response to one of his companions, and Korin couldn't hold back his own answering smile.

Varajas sighed. "I'll see you around, Korin." He slipped away over the rooftop. Korin hardly noticed.

Ádan was back.

ALSO BY BARBARA J. WEBB

The Invisible War

Midnight in St. Petersburg

Inquest

Apocrypha: The Dying World

City of Burning Shadows

What Dreams Shadows Cast